Downfallen

Book One of the Damascene Order

D1710330

Cover Art by Michael Schachtner

for Sandra

I

Ayyadieh 1191 A.D.

Vincent Kaverno had never before been given such an order. If not from the lips of the Lionheart Himself, even his fealty as Captain of the Guard may have wavered. But he had carried out his command, and three thousand lay slain unceremoniously.

He had witnessed more than his share of violence in this distant land, but this was more than bloodshed. This was wanton destruction and massacre. As his men dutifully cut down man, woman and child in full view of the enemy's headquarters, Vincent could not absently remove himself from the scene or deem this an honorable though disagreeable affair. Even as the inevitable, though ineffective, counterattack ensued and the King himself moved to retire, Vincent found his resolve and attachment to the campaign fading. He would complete this current tour with his men and then retire to England at the earliest juncture.

But there was one problem.

As his dirty surcoat turned from white to bright red, Vincent had felt a pull. The strokes of his battlesword rang dissonantly to the betraying of an inner honor. He felt as though an outer, unseen entity was condemning his actions and had passed judgment. When the killing field had drained its cup of lifeblood, the man who could claim honor now only in title wandered the reddened landscape as one detached from existence.

The pull became stronger.

Vincent threw his sword to the ground. He cast off his helmet and gauntlets, hardly needed for protection against civilians. Dark and ruddy features had been shadowed and ingrained with lines that denied his youth. Rubbing his eyes with his own flesh to remind himself of his humanity, Vincent realized that he had wandered far from the site of death. He looked up through tired eyes to see a singular wooden structure before him. Unknowingly, he had been walking for some time it seemed, but now he stopped and stood, bewildered.

The wooden structure was the source of the mysterious pull.

Vincent approached cautiously, for he recalled no such building in the vicinity prior to the order being given. It appeared to be a dwelling incongruously constructed apart and away from all other trappings of civilization. As he stood eying the meager outline that the home struck in the waning twilight, Vincent's attention was suddenly drawn toward a light burning from within the windowless walls. It pulsated, he realized, to the pace of his racing heart and shone out from the cracks and fissures between joints and planks. The dauntless Captain of the Guard ventured a shaking hand to push against the unadorned door when it swung open and inward in anticipation of his gesture.

A single-room dwelling greeted Vincent's senses, not nearly as uncommon as the placement of the structure itself, inhabited by a solitary figure who sat near a cold hearth opposite the door. The dweller was clearly an Easterner identifiably foreign to both Christian and Moor.

"Welcome, Vincent Kaverno of Ballecetine," he uttered in unwavering and clear English as he rose, referencing not only knowledge of Vincent's identity but also his origins.

Vincent remained a step behind the threshold, wary still and now perplexed.

"Yes, I do know who you are, Vincent," the foreigner continued, traversing the dwelling in five strides toward Vincent's right where a wooden case sat upon a utilitarian wrought iron table.

The speechless captain lowered his hand but did not venture entrance quite yet.

"Your presence here has been foretold. All things are as they must be."

"What do you know of things?" Vincent retorted, a bit harsher than intended.

At this, the unnamed Easterner looked up from the wooden case, but not toward Vincent. A wry smile crept across his face and his attention again turned downward.

"You are a man of blood, Vincent," he continued, "but you are not stained."

The captain stepped onto the threshold if nothing else than out of curiosity. There was one chair next to the hearth, and one table against the wall with the wooden case upon it. Three objects in a barren space and no more; not even the semblance of a food preparation nor sleeping area adorned its span.

"Who are you?" Vincent gasped, taking another bold step inward.

"It would do little good to tell you who I am, Vincent. But I am here to tell you about who you are."

Without hesitation, the mysterious foreigner lifted the case aloft and turned to face Vincent squarely. He held it outward in an obvious gesture that Vincent take it. Vincent allowed his gaze to rest upon the brass framing and clasps that held the two halves together. The case commanded an admirable span but yet seemed to be no more of a hindrance to the diminutive Easterner than a long feather; two hands were needed to balance the case but certainly not to support it.

Vincent corrected his earlier estimation; the pull was coming not from the structure, but the wooden case.

His caution overridden by curiosity, Vincent found himself holding the wooden case in two outstretched hands before consciously willing them to move and at that instant the scene changed in the blink of an eye. In a feeling that he could best approximate as waking suddenly from a deep sleep, Vincent shook physically and fully expected to find himself rising from a tense nap in his field tent. Only, he was still standing with the case in his hands and the wooden structure and enigmatic Easterner were not to be found.

Spinning in place, case still in hand, Vincent had no empirical explanation for what he had just witnessed. If not for the physical evidence of the encounter in his possession, he would have assumed it a passing hallucination from a conflicted and overworked psyche.

But here it was. The case. And it was in fact light as a feather.

Vincent knelt to the ground, setting the case to the side, and felt the ground where he knew the building to have been only moments ago. Then he allowed his hands to slide over the smooth wooden cover, tracing the metal rim in puzzlement.

"Captain," called a voice from behind.

Vincent rose hastily, leaving the case on the ground, and turned to face a sentry from among his ranks.

"His Majesty intends to leave at first light, and insists that you personally oversee preparations."

"Yes, very well," Vincent stammered, never truly focusing on the messenger. "Thank you."

After he was alone again, Vincent stared downward at the case. Without bending down to touch it, he could already sense the gravity that it commanded. It was the same sensation as before; an indistinct beckoning that seemed less from without and more from within. As the pragmatic Captain of the Guard wrestled with this abstract dilemma, he could tell that in the waning light of day a luminescence was emanating from the spaces between the halves of the box.

Something inexplicable and inescapably magnetic to his attention forced him back to his knees and in a moment he had flung open the lid to a momentary flood of the purest white light that he had ever witnessed. It was not blinding or debilitating in its intensity but was warm and permeating on a deeper level. After the initial wave, the brilliance subsided and Vincent could peer clearly into the slender and long container.

Within was the most elegant weapon he had yet beheld. A sword matching the proportions of a full two-handed blade lay diagonally from corner to corner of the wooden box wrapped in clean white rags so that only a silver crossguard and pommel were immediately visible. Leather straps secured the cloth around the blade, while loose fabric covered the handle. Vincent reached into the case and slid his hand under the cloth and onto the sword's hilt. It was cold to the touch, and more than cool in relation to the surroundings. As his hand moved the covering aside, a sculpted and superbly handcrafted ivory handle greeted his senses, and his dominant hand flew toward it. Again, as before in the foreigner's house, his body acted before his mind could fully take in the situation and Vincent found himself holding the covered blade aloft. The carving of the handle, thickness, and feel of the silver fittings all fit his hand as though it had been built to his exact specifications. What amazed the experienced Captain the most, however, was not the expert craftsmanship or aesthetic appeal of the blade but its superior lack of weight or heft that a weapon of its stature should surely command. He stood, easily wielding the longsword with one hand. With two, unearthly and terrible blows would be possible.

Vincent decided that he needed to see if the same attention to detail carried through to the weapon's most critical function. Upon loosening the ties around the blade, he left the covering fall to the ground and saw flawless Damascus steel, four full feet long on its own, terminating in a deadly point that looked never to have seen combat; the entire weapon appeared clean from the blacksmith's shop and not a nick nor blemish marred its blade and fittings. Vincent knew the mystery, strength and legend surrounding the tempestuous patterns and lines along the length of the blade and understood at once that this could not have been a weapon owned by any but the highest nobility of the land. Saladin himself would have been proud to lay claim to this worthy blade, though its pattern and style were European and not indigenous.

The light was fading quickly now, and Vincent began to fear dereliction of his duties if he were to linger much longer at the present site. He hastily, and reluctantly, wrapped the blade and secured it in its case, but the longer it remained not in his grasp the stronger the pull became. Vincent stopped after a few steps to a strange tingling in his fingertips and realized that the sensation was not unique at all but merely the familiar waking of an extremity gone numb from cold. He recalled that the sword had seemed unnaturally cool to the touch, but then lost track of his senses in his rapture of the blade itself. In the few moments that his hands were in contact with the handle, they had ceased to be his hands; they were somehow connected to the weapon and the weightlessness that it had exhibited was less from lack of mass but more because it was a part of him. It felt no heavier or lighter than his flesh and bone simply because it was, in effect, a direct extension of his arm.

Vincent could see his discarded battlesword just ahead. He was about to start out to retrieve his equipment when the receding light caused a glint of metal to reflect from the underside of the wooden case. Not having examined the lower portion of the box, he turned it over and saw that a brass plate had been affixed in the center of the case's backside. It bore an inscription:

The four Archangels are always keen
Of he who bears dread Damascene

He let the words roll over in his mind. *Archangels. Damascene.* Archangels were powerful heavenly beings, that much Vincent knew. Damascene could only refer to the blade within. Damascus steel was not uncommon in this foreign land, but the marriage of it and the Western-styled weapon at his side was an incongruity. He did have to admit earlier, while carrying out his gruesome task, that an uneasy feeling had overtaken him and it was not simply revulsion at the work itself; in perspective and with time to reflect upon it more fully, Vincent became more and more convinced that he had not only committed a sin against his conscience but also against something greater than himself. It was this realization in the growing twilight that caused the greatest anxiety in the mind of the Captain from Ballecetine.

Morning came early to the sleepless captain. By sunrise, he was directing supplies onto transport ships and before the sun had reached the apex of its ascent Vincent Kaverno was on board his own vessel headed west. It was substantially more difficult than it should have been to relinquish the wooden case to the cargo hold below, but he comforted himself in the knowledge that most of the knights in his company had also procured various items and trinkets as souvenirs of their arduous, though ultimately failed, expedition.

He knew that several knights from his home principality were also headed home, and a few were certain to be in his company on board. Altogether, five transports left in this, the first wave of returning men. There would be many more but the King himself had insisted that Vincent bring the vanguard out and set the pace.

"You know, when my grandfather returned from the Great Crusade, it was to a hero's welcome," called an immediately recognized voice from the stern. "What do you think awaits us?"

Vincent did not have to turn to identify the origin of the voice; he knew it to be Martin Cleahim, fellow knight of the same allegiance as he.

"Who writes the history of this campaign will remember our resolve, but we will be remembered, that much is certain," Vincent responded as the duo embraced mightily on the ascent to the ship's forecastle.

Martin stood fully three inches taller than Vincent, which in itself was a rarity, and commanded a considerably formidable presence, having a more muscular frame than the sinewy captain. The two knights had grown up together in the principality of Ballecetine and, being very close in age, found service under Lord West and had been knighted with the same blade. Those viewing the reunion of the pair would have noted a peculiar twist, however, on the customary greeting of knights from this region. Whereas it was common practice to grasp the right elbow with one's right hand and embrace with the left arm, pulling the other close and touching the other's right elbow to the heart, this pair did so in mirror likeness; they embraced with the right arm and grasped the left elbow. This was because, as any in the principality knew, Martin was wrong-handed and it was a show of respect from the captain to his most trusted ally.

"It is not *that* we will be remembered, but *how*," the left-handed knight remarked as they released and walked out toward the bow of the lead ship.

"We will have little control over that I'm afraid," Vincent concluded.

It was also plainly evident upon casual observation that Martin relished surrounding himself with full battle regalia when many in the company had dressed down in the absence of battlefield urgency. This had been true even in the heat of the longest marches and harshly unfamiliar climate that they were at that moment leaving behind. While others had shed armor or succumbed, Martin had held the pace and bore the load unceasingly. Even now Vincent knew his mantle and mail shirt to lie just beneath the blue tunic while the captain himself wore no armor at all and felt quite comfortable in this freedom.

Vincent did allow himself one extravagance, though, and it hung around his neck on a silver chain, hidden except to those who knew him well.

"Perhaps Lord West will grant you her favor after our return," Martin suggested, knowing also that which his close friend kept closest to his heart. "Which was the plan all along?"

Vincent allowed himself a slight smile, knowing the spirit that Martin intended.

"What happened to Sir Mills of Elben, after attempting to court without following proper channels?" Martin continued.

The wind picked up as the ships gained speed, causing the silver pendant that called out Vincent's transgression to bounce freely against his loosely-fitted shirt. He raised his right hand to his heart, pulling the bauble along, and remembered again, as he had countless times in the past three years, the details of their last meeting before his departure.

It was not uncommon for a knight departing for war to seek the favor of a maiden, for Vincent personally knew several men now heading homeward for whom this was a primary motivation to return whole, but he doubted greatly that any had vowed unswerving loyalty to the Lord of Ballecetine's only offspring and daughter, Diana West. This he had done, and they had sealed the engagement by exchanging small items that represented their respective family's lineage. Vincent had given Diana a miniature chisel carved by himself out of bone, as his father was a stonecutter. Lord West's daughter, in return, had given him a minuscule yet intricately sculpted silver dragon that hung near Vincent's heart at all times, as the silver dragon was a primary symbol of the West family crest. This sort of exchange was commonplace among the well-to-do of the realm, but always between consenting parents of the betrothed either with or without the intended couple's knowledge or assent. It was not, as Vincent and Diana had done, a contract to be made under moonlight in secret and in the absence of a father's blessing, especially when the patriarch in question was an eminent potentate of a vast and powerful domain.

"I'm sure you will fare much better," Martin continued, the third of three souls with knowledge of the illicit agreement. "The search for a new captain would certainly prove difficult in these times."

"That is the key to success in many situations," Vincent jibed, "make yourself valuable enough to your superiors as to cause the cost of replacing you seem preposterous."

The two shared a good laugh on the forward section of the ship, and the sun began to set ahead. Vincent knew this to be but the first leg of their return, but already each minute brought him closer to home, and her.

In the darkening belowdeck of Vincent's transport, the innocuous wooden case which held an artifact of untold worth began to glow a faint, but distinct white light.

"Captain!" came the shout from the lookout post above.

Instantly, both Vincent and Martin spun toward the center of the ship, casting their attention upward.

"Three, no, four pirate galleys close!" came the reply. The lookout pointed ahead and to the left, but Vincent could not see them because of the ships in formation about them and the blinding sunset, which he knew to be by design.

"No rest for the weary," Martin quipped as Vincent rounded up the crew and they began to arm themselves with longbows.

Vincent had anticipated rough sailing at some point on their journey, but this soon couldn't be a coincidence. There had to be some reason for harassing crusader traffic so quickly after departure. No matter, the wily captain had made sure each vessel in the group had an ample supply of ranged weapons to hold enemies at bay.

Similar cries went up from the flanking ships, and in mere moments each vessel was manned by longbowmen with arrows ready, but the issue at hand was not able and willing defenders; the sun was at the precise angle as to completely frustrate the crusaders' aim and visibility in the advent of the attack.

"Turn us away from the sun!" Vincent shouted to the helmsman.

The transport lazily listed to its right, a maneuver that the other vessels on that side also adopted, but they were too slow compared to the sleek design and maneuverability of the closing ships. The sickening clamor of splintering wood and shouts filled the air momentarily and it was then that Vincent knew the intent of the approaching fleet was not simply to demand tribute or parlay for passage. His ship was the first to clear the sun's effect and as they looked upon the scene ahead Vincent's fears were substantiated. The lead galley had been affixed with a ram and had impaled the wide and exposed hull of one of the transports. The oarsmen were reversing to maximize damage and accelerate the ship's fate, a tactic that was well-known to be sure, but what puzzled Vincent the most was that the other galleys did not move in to board the wounded ship. They simply stayed behind as though the objective of the mission were to inflict punitive damage.

"What are they doing?" Martin cried out, himself raising a longbow and waiting for the command to fire.

The ship that had been between Vincent's and the unfortunate first target had continued straight ahead and been left unmolested though the other galleys could surely have caught up to it if they had wished. This created a face-off between the pirate group and Vincent's transport and, as the lead galley pulled free of its first victim, Vincent gave the command to fire and dozens of arrows flew true to target.

The results were mixed, as the galley crew had also anticipated this defense and had raised several large wooden shields to minimize casualties from a frontal counterattack. As his longbowmen rearmed, Vincent calculated that they would have one or possibly two more rounds of fire until the ram came to their ship, which it doubtlessly was as they could hear the rowing commands prod the men to full speed and the prow of the galley straightened and began accelerating forward again.

The damaged transport was taking on water fast, and its crew had largely abandoned ship save for one figure that broke the flaming horizon. As the second volley flew, the single figure on the sinking vessel fired an arrow into the undefended backside of the charging galley, then a second flew with swift precision. This did not cause the galley to slow its approach, but it did open a window of fire as one of the precious shields fell upon the second stroke.

This was all the opportunity the crusader archers needed, as the other two ships now rejoined Vincent's and a flurry of arrows funneled toward the breach in the enemy's armor. Even though only a small proportion hit the exact target and reaped heavy losses, the momentum of the speeding vessel caused it to still impact the lead transport with sufficient force to wedge itself securely into the hull, splitting the keel and compromising the forecastle upon which Vincent and a few other men stood.

The forward structure crumpled as the galley came to a halt and confusion reigned. The support galleys were racing to join the fray, as this transport was the focal point of their foray. Vincent and two archers by his side fell headlong onto one of the still raised wooden shields and slid swiftly down the incline and into the sea.

Martin and the others managed to maintain their balance and drew weapons to defend the damaged vessel as the remaining crew of the battering galley made to board.

Vincent swam beneath the sinking ship, his only thought being the Damascus Sword in the forward cargo hold. As he forced his mind to recall the case's exact location, bodies began falling into the water behind him; the melee on deck had begun. He had no time to learn the identities of the fallen men as either friend or foe because his lungs, unprepared for the dive, were reaching their limit. He had to surface and come down again, but the transport was sinking swiftly. Then, in the decisive moment between life and death, his quick mind struck on a compromise. Vincent swiftly swam into the gaping hole in the side of his vessel and surfaced within the quickly filling cargo hold and accomplished both his objectives; lungs filled again and the wooden case floated but an arm's reach from his location.

Finding the buoyant treasure amid the raucous fray above, Vincent planned to immediately open the case and abandon it in favor of its contents. Shouts, pounding and cries filled his draining ears as full use of his senses returned if only temporarily before he must again dive into the cold expanse. The ceiling of the hold was rapidly sinking toward him, and but a few more deep breaths would be possible before he must brave the sea to attempt escape. His urge to live compounded with steeled military resolve and just as Vincent's hand touched the wooden case he became distantly aware of a faint pulsating rhythm in his chest which he immediately dismissed as only his racing heartbeat. He began to question this phenomenon as the case sprung open, revealing a dazzling and reverberating cadence of blinding light emanating from the fiery pattern on the Damascus Sword's blade in precise time to the pounding within his chest. The water had risen to his chin and the case's open cover contacted the deck above just as his right hand touched the intricate ivory handle and the world faded to black around him.

Vincent's eyes opened to a sparse and desolate land not unlike the harsh climate of his present campaign far from home. He knew enough to tell that this must be a dream or hallucination of some sort, perhaps the wandering of a drowning and delirious mind, but he also felt immediately safe and inexplicably secure. The sun was high, and the horizon barren and distant. In the haze of the midday's heat he thought he saw a figure standing off in the distance, or was it just a mirage?

Vincent began walking toward the figure, which seemed to be standing still and facing him almost expectantly. When he reached close enough proximity to identify features and characteristics, the mysterious figure disappeared. Vincent halted and scanned his surroundings. For the first time, he looked down and saw that he was clothed in civilian attire, bereft entirely of weapon or defense. As he took stock of his situation, a glimmer caught his attention on the periphery of his vision. It was the figure again, this time far off to his right at roughly the same range as it had been the first time. With hardly any alternative course of action, Vincent turned and began to walk toward the outline once more. The results were identical. Again, just as he thought he could begin to discern finer detail, it was gone.

Feeling a twinge of frustration, Vincent looked all about the horizon and saw the shape coalesce this time much closer than it had been the first two times. He could tell that the shape was female. She stayed corporeal and stationary this time, which hastened Vincent's approach. The unnamed stranger was tall and slender but obscured by a flowing green garment and opaque veil. Vincent stood at arm's length from the unspeaking and unmoving form. His first instinct was to reach out and remove the veil, but he thought better of it and chose to address the female instead.

"Who are you?"

He could not tell if the person had heard him, for no body posturing or receptive gestures accompanied his question. As he stood awkwardly awaiting an answer, Vincent noticed that the garment seemed to be flowing around the form in an undulating and fluid-like state rather than touching or following the contours of the individual beneath. Just as his hands rose to lift the veil, an ethereal and articulate response issued forth.

"*Deceivers four have sworn again to plant the Seed in honored men.*"

The reply was cryptic enough to cause Vincent pause, and it was in that instant of hesitation that the form wisped away as smoke, slipping through the captain's extended fingers as he reached out, too late.

II

A gasp and wrenching spasm of the first inhalation of seawater called Vincent back into reality. Whatever phenomenon he had just experienced would have to await examination at some later point as personal survival took the forefront of his faculties.

The Damascus Sword, or *Damascene,* was firmly in his grasp and Vincent took one last deep breath and plunged into the water, exiting the sinking cargo hold and as soon as he was able, ascending to the surface. The scene above beckoned him and the captain climbed the broken hull of his vessel to join the battle, waterlogged and heavy but willing and empowered by the brand in his possession.

As he rose to the plane of battle upon the skewed deck of his tilting transport, Vincent joined the cause and the Damascus Sword flew with celerity. The glowing sword did not discern limb nor blade; cleaving and slashing toward the center of the doomed ship, Vincent felt a stirring within multiplied many times over as the cold ivory handle ceased to be a simple instrument in his hand.

It had become a part of him.

The sight of the resurgent captain wielding an unearthly, glowing weapon was impetus to convince the remaining boarding party to retreat. Within moments, the battering-ram equipped galley had pulled free but the conflict was far from over. The initial transport that had been rammed was now nowhere to be seen, the lone valiant archer's fate a mystery, and Vincent's transport dipped sufficiently low as to cause the remaining crew to evacuate to the sea and make for the closest undamaged vessel.

In the confusion, Vincent had lost contact with Martin but counted this as trivial as they had undoubtedly survived far greater trials in their time together in this foreign land. What was more urgent was the state of the fleet now outnumbered with no seeming answer for the enemy's tactics.

The galley that had rammed both transports was preparing for its run on the next target. Vincent wondered what their objective might be. It was not to plunder the crusader vessels, as any cargo save the Damascus Sword was soon to be upon the seafloor. As he watched the stern of his transport sink below the surface, Vincent caught sight of a lone figure climbing onto the enemy flagship. He had a longbow slung over one shoulder and a trio of arrows clamped between his teeth. The captain began to swim toward the galley at best speed to aid the invasion, and as he approached spied a small group of his displaced shipmates drawing the same conclusion and reaching the galley just as the lone archer ascended to the deck and loosed his first arrow into the unsuspecting back of the helmsman. The second and third flew as lightning into the next pair of ambushed crewmen and as the galley began to list for lack of guidance, Vincent held hope that he could yet intercept it as it drifted obliquely away.

It was at that moment that Martin and one other ally had completed scaling the opposite side of the vessel and emerged atop, scoring a decisive and swift victory. Vincent arrived on the scene momentarily and four crusaders now stood in possession of the lead galley. The others could still be seen rowing away briskly, apparently having lost their will to carry on the offensive without their primary weapon.

"Captain," one of the knights addressed as Vincent stood among them. All eyes were upon the glowing blade in his hand.

"Well done, all," Vincent responded, as straggling knights from the cold sea found safety on the surrounding transports, which had by now circled close to the captured galley. He made a point to turn toward the valiant one who had initiated the strategy and, Vincent suspected, was also the lone archer who had aided the assault as his vessel sank beneath him.

"I am Captain Vincent Kaverno of Ballecetine," he introduced himself, extending his right hand after shifting the Damascus Sword to his left.

"James Laphrea," the archer responded and, as he detected the silence that indicated he was to complete his introduction, continued, "for hire."

"I see," Vincent replied, releasing his grasp. "Then, James Laphrea, consider yourself employed by myself for the remainder of this journey."

James nodded in compliant assurance.

Vincent then turned toward the man who had accompanied Martin in the ambush from the far side of the galley.

"William Reilu," he offered, sheathing his battlesword, "of Gallifrey."

Vincent extended his hand to him as well, thanking him for his service.

"Martin Laphrea," Martin concluded, "also of Ballecetine."

The foursome stood in a silence punctuated only by the distress of the captives below them manning the oars.

"The men below should be taken to the nearest port," Martin suggested, eyes fixed upon the glowing brand at his captain's side, and then to the right hand that had until recently wielded the sword. "Captain . . ." he trailed.

Vincent held up his right hand to the realization that he could not feel the extremity from fingertip to elbow and that the affected area had turned a sickly pale shade of blue.

"What is it?" James mused, wide-eyed.

Vincent's gaze shifted to the sword in his left hand, which he quickly dropped to the deck, still glowing intensely for what purpose he knew not.

"I can't feel my arm," he answered, flexing the tendons and muscles affected. He still had full range of motion and use of his sword arm, but no sensation of any kind.

Martin strode to his side, bending low to examine the sword. He reached out with his dominant left hand to touch the handle and, as he did, jumped back grasping it in pain. William and James leaped subtly in surprise as Martin fell to the deck, and were at his side immediately. Vincent approached and crouched in bewilderment. Martin's hand had become traced with pale blue lines that started at his fingertips and faded near his wrist. After the initial shock, which was intense and unpleasant, Martin commented that his hand felt as though he had lost feeling but it returned gradually over the following few moments. The four knights encircled the Damascus Sword warily, as though it might become animated and attack them at any moment.

"Where did you find this?" Martin asked.

"That is part of the mystery," the captain replied, eyeing the glowing, pulsating rhythm of the blade closely. "After the slaughter, I was led to a cabin where . . . an old man gave it to me."

Even as he spoke, Vincent realized the ridiculousness of his exposition, but it was the truth and he continued amid the sideways glances of his allies who split their attention between his retelling and the artifact upon the wooden deck.

"I can't explain it," Vincent abruptly concluded. He did not include the details regarding the cabin seeming to disappear and his subsequent vision while in the cargo hold.

"It is Damascus steel," William quipped, appearing to want nothing more than to touch the flawlessly crafted blade but knowing better.

James, in daring fashion, poked at the sword with the tip of his longbow as though to provoke a response. Then he retracted his weapon and touched the area that had made contact with the sword. It seemed unaffected.

"It only affects flesh," Martin stated, flexing his left hand and feeling full sensation in it once more. Vincent's arm was returning to normal, he could tell, but much more slowly. "And it only seems to want you to touch it," he added, gesturing toward his captain.

Vincent bent over the blade, reaching out both hands and letting them hover closely. He could not sense any abnormal effects short of making physical contact with the sword itself, so he used his surcoat as a barrier and lifted it aloft. At a loss as to a long-term solution, since the wooden case had perished with the rest of the cargo on his transport, Vincent cradled the lengthy weapon with his covered left hand upon the hilt so that the blade rested against his arm and shoulder pointing upward.

The four knights dispersed belowdeck and made a quick survey of the chained men manning the oars. There were a dozen rows of oarsmen, one on each side of the vessel. This created an immediate problem as space on the three remaining transports was already at a premium since they were being required to absorb the crews of the two ill-fated crusader ships; two dozen more individuals of diverse motives and backgrounds would hardly make for an amicable return journey.

Martin and Vincent conversed briefly on the topic and concluded that they would bear the added strain of the extra men only until the next port presented itself. They were systematically released from their bonds and divided equally among the three transports being generally thankful for their fortune at falling into the hands of crusader traffic. From what Vincent could surmise of their makeup they were mostly captured locals and perhaps a handful were prisoners of war. They were able-bodied and could contribute to their respective vessels, save for one incongruous figure who made his way with considerable difficulty and strain. Vincent walked up to the man, the last one to evacuate, and addressed him.

"How is it that you came to be upon this vessel?" he inquired. The final captive was considerably older than the rest and visibly frail.

The old man looked toward Vincent but not at him directly. He was eyeing the Damascus Sword, which had not dulled in its supernatural brilliance the entire time since Vincent had retrieved it from the cargo hold.

"I am here because of you, Vincent," the elderly man answered with a clarity and force that denied his outer appearance.

The two of them were alone and Vincent did not know exactly how to respond. At first, the fact that he had addressed him by name seemed strange, but he certainly could have overheard it at some point during the boarding and strategizing stage of their situation. What unnerved him the most was not the content but the certainty with which he spoke.

"How do you know who I am?" Vincent stalled, turning so that his body shielded the Damascus Sword from his unfaltering gaze.

Vincent's strategy worked, and the old man looked the captain in the eye now as he spoke. "I am here because of you, and for you, Vincent. You are my son."

At this, Vincent took the man to be a lunatic and laughed out loud for the first time he could remember in quite a while. Not only was his father alive and well back in Ballecetine to the best of his knowledge, but the man before him was also more than a few decades the elder to his actual patriarch. Vincent turned to leave, not sure if he should be relieved at the inane nature of the old man's claim or concerned for his sanity among the other crew members.

"If you doubt me, son," the old man shot with force that caused Vincent to halt and face him sideways for a tense moment, "then believe me when I tell you that sword will be your destruction!"

Vincent looked to the still glowing blade cradled in his left arm and then squared off toward the old man. "What do you know of the sword?"

The old man smiled a gapped grin, creases edging his languished features. He said nothing. Vincent approached to arm's length, noting how the proximity of the Damascus Sword elicited an increasingly concerned visage upon his smug features.

"Perhaps you would like to experience its effect," the captain added, moving to grasp the cold ivory handle but hoping not to be required to fulfill his bluff as feeling had just recently returned completely.

"No," the man pleaded, shrinking from the advancing captain and holding up his hands.

"We will speak of this more, old man," Vincent seethed, sensing that the situation about them would not allow for a detailed explanation. It was no matter, Vincent surmised, as they would have a great deal of time to converse on the way to the nearest port. He left for the main deck and the old man exited to a nearby transport.

Martin, William and James had taken up residence upon Vincent's newly commandeered transport. The captain noted that the old man also was housed within, which brought a sense of security as his rantings would not be a hindrance to others. He shifted the Damascus Sword uneasily, sensing the numbing cold quality to be seeping through the cloth barrier. He needed to be able to deposit the blade somewhere remote but yet secure. As he mulled this over, Martin approached with a dilemma.

"We are at a loss as to what to do with the captured galley," he explained. "Some of us believe that it could be an asset on the remainder of the journey."

"What do you think?" Vincent countered.

Martin looked pensively toward the bobbing and empty vessel. "If we were to man it with a skeleton crew, it might be able to keep pace well enough even though its sail is small."

The thought had not occurred to the honorable men to force the oarsmen into another tour of labor simply to facilitate their speed; all were in agreement that the captives were to contribute to the operation of the remaining ships but would be accorded the basic rights of passengers otherwise. Vincent's face brightened as he and his closest ally shared a moment of clarity.

The fleet of three with the addition of one captured vessel struck out onto the waters after a minor crew reassignment. The exceptionally light and nimble galley, having been relieved of its drag-inducing unmanned oars, led the group. Its crew numbered four and at the prow stood the homeward captain of the guard.

III

The following several days passed with relative ease. No further engagements with enemy ships presented themselves, and the four knights who manned the commandeered galley piloted the fleet swiftly toward an agreed-upon destination: the Templar held port city of Iden. It would be three more day's journey, during which time the captain made regular visits to the trailing transports to make sure the overloaded vessels were managing with twice as many men and half the needed supplies. He purposely avoided the old man who claimed him as his son.

"I have not heard of the principality of Gallifrey," James posited toward the group, but specifically toward William, during one of the group's afternoon meals out on the open deck. These informal meetings had become commonplace as the four knights formed an unspoken bond in the short time that some of them had known each other.

"It is an eastern coastal land," Martin supplied, preparing a freshly-caught fish for the hot coals that resided in the makeshift oven. To ease the burden, the four had determined to requisition what supplies and sustenance they required from either the galley stores or the sea itself. For veteran knights accustomed to the field it was a small adjustment and retained a semblance of autonomy amid the confines of a wooden hull.

"Yes," William concurred. "It is small and agricultural, with few aspirations toward imperialist tendencies."

Vincent smiled and Martin shook his head as both detected the subtle slight cast toward their homeland of Ballecetine, which was known far beyond its outposted perimeter as an aggressively expansionist power. At least Gallifrey and Ballecetine had never come into conflict so far as Vincent understood his regional history.

"Do you have family there?" James continued.

William seemed a bit uncomfortable discussing details of his personal life, which made sense to the ever perceptive captain. For all his initiative in aiding the capture of the vessel they currently called home, William was far more comfortable examining the inanimate elements of the tangible such as the mechanicals of the galley's rigging and superstructure. The past two nights while Vincent had taken the watch, William had uneasily paced and inspected the deck and perimeter of the ship and had participated little in conversation or exposition. This was in direct contrast to the archer knight who seemingly wanted to know everything about everyone and passed his time not in silent reflection or contemplative pacing but in repetitive target practice and an eagerness for a break to the monotony that Vincent could sympathize with but also curb effectively in favor of solitude.

"I have no maiden in waiting if that is what you suggest," William countered. "Do you have the tension set yet?"

Vincent detected the masterful deflection of the silent knight as he accepted a parcel from Martin hot off the flame. William and James were a walking contradiction, but there was one intersection in their often conflicting personalities: weaponry. James had discovered a crossbow among the miscellany in the galley's stores in need of repair and, since the quiet knight relished a challenge of the tactile sort and the archer knight enjoyed shooting things with ranged artillery, a synthesis was reached. The two of them disappeared belowdeck with childlike alacrity, leaving the Ballecetine contingent above to enjoy the elements.

Martin's gaze flew immediately to the Damascus Sword, which stood reverently against the mast since being deposited there by the captain upon the claiming of the vessel. Its blade still glowed, though not as vibrantly as it had during the battle and subsequent boarding of the galley. Martin thought at one point that perhaps its aura was a reflection of the setting sun always ahead of them, but upon further inspection the odd effect remained a mystery.

"I cannot determine the nature of this light," Vincent lamented, standing and walking toward the sword as Martin followed closely. The two knights stared, at a complete loss, when the glow dissipated instantly, like a flame immediately quenched.

Martin looked in astonishment to Vincent, who returned an expression of puzzled concern. The captain reached out a hand and touched the now naturally luminescent metal surface of the blade and, feeling no strange effects or numbing cold, took hold of the handle and raised the sword. It still exhibited an unnatural lack of mass as he swung it in slow circles but otherwise seemed a curiously normal piece of equipment. Martin, the consummate swordsman of the realm, seemed eager and yet respectful as Vincent eyed the surfaces closely in the waning light of day.

"Do you think the painful sensation will be gone now that the blade is no longer glowing?" Vincent posed, holding the sword toward Martin.

Martin reached out instantly then paused. "I suppose there is one way to find out," he hesitantly answered.

Vincent backed slightly, extending his reach. Martin allowed his weaker right hand to approach, hover, and then light first upon the ivory handle of the magnificent weapon. Fingertips made contact, with no adverse effects. Feeling brave, Martin grasped with his non-dominant hand and lifted the Damascus Sword from Vincent's support. Observing Vincent wave the blade easily with one hand gave Martin false confidence, as it immediately fell to the deck once he had its entire heft in his possession.

Slightly embarrassed, Martin bent to retrieve the blade, being required to use both hands and a proportionally great amount of effort to lift it. He was able to swing the great sword but it seemed obstinately massive and awkwardly unbalanced in his possession. Martin felt that the sword was refusing to allow him to hold it. He shook his head in utter bewilderment, handing it back to his captain, in whose possession it seemed weightless.

It was at that moment that Vincent noticed activity on the deck of the transport nearest them. There was a great commotion and waving of arms and shouting directed toward the galley which both Martin and Vincent traversed the length of the vessel to investigate immediately. Several of the former galley oarsmen and a few of the crusader contingent were overlapping and interrupting each other, nearly falling into the sea at the bow of the ship to relay some news of obvious import.

William and James emerged from below, carrying a wooden contraption between the two of them, just in time to assume command of the galley as both Martin and Vincent boarded the nearby transport after it had approached and lowered a bridge. Vincent had the Damascus Sword in hand, but only due to his and Martin's examination of its lack of luminescence.

"What is it?" Vincent demanded, as from appearances the entire complement of the vessel had assembled on deck. Everyone, but one.

"It is the old man," one fellow crusader supplied. "He . . . disappeared."

"What do you mean?" Vincent retorted. "Did he go overboard?"

"No, sir," the man attempted to clarify. "He simply . . . vanished."

Martin and Vincent seemed much less astounded by the report than the rest of the crew had expected.

"Did this occur only a few moments ago, as the sun was setting?" Martin questioned.

"Yes, exactly then," the confused crusader answered.

Vincent and Martin shared a knowing look.

"It was at the same moment that the blade stopped glowing," Vincent surmised, holding the sword up to scrutiny. "It glowed from the time the enemy ships attacked, with the old man present, until he left."

"Somehow, the old man is connected to the sword," Martin added.

"Yes," Vincent concluded. "And he believes that I am his son."

This he spoke lowly, though Martin had been privy to the information as part of their conversation in past days.

The conclusion was reached that the crew should head back to their stations, with no concrete answer to the oddity that they had witnessed. Some who had not directly seen the occurrence blamed fatigue from the campaign and lack of rest, which was certainly true, but a stalwart segment of the crew denied any consoling words and sat in defiance to anything that would discount their report. It was twilight, and Vincent headed back to the galley with Martin close behind.

William and James were sitting on the deck with what appeared to be a crossbow lying in pieces between them. One would hold the implement steady while the other tightened or bent some protuberance and then they would switch positions and the other would steady the device. Martin and Vincent stood in silent admiration for several moments before James spoke up.

"We've designed a heavy dual crossbow," he stated, lifting a massive wooden device to scrutiny.

"It has some . . . issues to be worked out," William offered, placing his hand upon the frame of the barely-recognizable weapon. "But we are confident that by the time we make landfall it should be ready for use."

Vincent at first meant to question what type of confrontation they had been anticipating to warrant such a tactic, but then thought better of cutting down the two knights' apparent mechanism for coping with the journey. He managed a genuine smile as he reached out to examine the magnificent invention of the resourceful duo, setting the Damascus Sword aside.

"This is," he began with little expectation then became increasingly fascinated, "truly remarkable."

Martin leaned in to take in the sight and the two rotated and examined the implement closely for several moments. The heft of the necessary structure rendered the weapon terribly bulky, but Vincent immediately understood the mindset and rationale underpinning the design. He handed it back to an expectant James, who seemed satisfied at the level of attention it had garnered.

The sun had now set and an eerie darkness overtook the small fleet. William and James were content with the weak glow of the coals to carry on their work, while Martin descended belowdeck. Vincent took up the Damascus Sword and strode to the prow.

What was the meaning of the old man from the galley? He knew Vincent by name and had apparent knowledge of the Damascus Sword. His disappearance and the coinciding darkening of the blade could not have been by chance; there was a connection between the two events. Resting with his back against the bulkhead, the captain of the guard set the blade upon the deck and allowed himself a moment of repose. He closed his eyes and let his mind wander to the homeland that he knew so well yet still so far away. Always, she was there. Would she remember him as he had remembered her? Vincent reached beneath his tunic and slid the silver pendant up and over his head to examine it for the hundredth time since departing Ballecetine. The silver dragon, intricately carved and detailed, held him in rapture as it always had, though this time another sensation accompanied his musings. A wave of exhaustion overtook him to which he graciously succumbed and slumped against the wooden battlement.

Vincent's eyes snapped open but it was to debilitating darkness so palpable that he initially thought himself blind. Startled and disoriented, he attempted to stand but found that he could not discern his surroundings. The constant motion of sea travel was not present; Vincent understood at that moment that he was dreaming but his senses were sharper and more present than in any dream he had ever experienced.

He is here.

A whisper as close as his ear called.

Instinctively, Vincent spun and reached out for the origin of the voice. Only empty air passed through his grasp.

We only have moments.

A second, but similar voice.

Both were female, but Vincent could not pinpoint their location. It was then that he concluded that the voices were not from his surroundings but were within his mind.

"Who are you?" Vincent shouted.

In response, a piercing cold shot through his body, paralyzing and stiffening him immediately. In his numbing torment, Vincent knew this dreamlike sensation to be the same as before when he had encountered the mysterious figure in his vision while retrieving the Damascus Sword from the cargo hold. Every muscle in his body tensed and convulsed but he fought the urge to awaken in anticipation of learning more of the voices.

He will soon know the cost.

The first voice again.

Vincent sensed himself slipping away, back to reality but pushed it away.

He is not strong enough.

The silver dragon pendant had fallen to the deck, and it was Vincent's first waking action to don it again. Uncertain of the events he had just witnessed, he spent the last few moments of dusk in quiet contemplation, all the while concentrating on the serene surface of the Damascus Sword as though it could impart some clarity to the confused captain.

IV

Four vessels broke the horizon, attracting the immediate attention of the Templar guard stationed at the port city of Iden. Three were recognized at once as crusader traffic but the lead galley was not as received until Vincent and three accompanying knights who bore the cross could be seen piloting the craft.

Vincent had secured the Damascus Sword in a thick cloth, wrapping the blade and hilt completely before strapping it onto his back so that only the ivory handle and silver pommel extended above his right shoulder. Still, it was a conspicuous piece judging simply by its length, but the captain sought to consult an authority in relics on their short stay at the allied town.

Martin and Vincent stepped from the captured galley, while William and James departed separately into the thoroughfare. Arrangements were to depart at first light the next day, and the contingent of all four ships dispersed inland as attending knights escorted the former galley captives back to shore.

A village of makeshift tents and lean-to constructions dominated the immediate coastal vicinity with the more permanent dwellings and Templar-run official locales farther inland. Vincent and Martin made their way briskly through the outer rim and commotion, finding an inroad quickly.

Upon inquiring along the way, the duo learned of a man named Breagil who had been among the initial wave of crusaders but had not ventured as far as the others toward the Holy Land. He had instead devoted his energy toward the charity and service of those who sought to complete the journey. Breagil himself had become well-versed in relics and symbolisms, both genuine and invented, and Vincent hoped that he could shed lucidity upon the Damascus Sword.

Vincent found himself continually casting his gaze over his shoulder or sliding a hand behind to reassure himself that the sword still hung from his back as its deceptive lack of heft denied its size and awkwardness in the bustling activity of the path. He had not considered carrying a more accessible sidearm as they had disembarked and carried no weapon at all save the magnificent, though hindered, blade. This omission was quelled by his knowledge that the knight to his left carried no fewer than five or six efficiently retrievable weapons upon various access points. Should combat become a necessity for whatever reason within the confines of Iden, Vincent could think of no ally more formidable than the foremost swordsman in all of Ballecetine.

To an innocuous observer, the two ambled somewhat recklessly along the way but experience and presence of mind had instilled in them the habit of the captain always taking the right and Martin the left. This was to play to the strong hand of each and non-interference with the other's sword arm in the case of a sudden confrontation.

Civilian and soldier alike filled the pathways and business routes into and out of Iden. It was the closest stopping point from the crusader principalities of the East, and dangerously so as evidenced by the high proportion of armed escorts and men-at-arms that lined its roads. Vincent and Martin came to a field tent matching the description given to them about the man who could perhaps unravel the mysteries of Vincent's relic. The opening waved freely in the breeze, and Vincent strode into the threshold to find a solitary man working with his back to them.

"Yes, come in please," invited the inhabitant, still not turning from his work.

"Are you Breagil?" Vincent asked before venturing any farther.

The man turned and faced them, nodding in the affirmative and walking towards the pair but instantly fixing his eyes over Vincent's right shoulder. For some reason, Martin expected more of a sagely presence, but Breagil seemed to be junior to himself and the captain, perhaps by several years.

"Breagil is my family name, you may call me Robert," he introduced, stopping at three or four pace's distance.

"Very well, Robert," Vincent answered, sliding the leather strap of the Damascus Sword from his shoulder. "I have found this artifact in the Holy Land, near Acre."

At this point Vincent held the weapon outward tentatively.

"I have been told that you have much knowledge of relics and artifacts," he finished, as Robert eyed the blade closely and Vincent carefully slid the blade from its protective covering.

"Damascus Steel," he whispered in awe.

"It has a strange effect that we have both witnessed," Vincent continued.

"Has this blade seen combat?" Robert asked with punctuated disbelief.

"Only one brief encounter with pirates while in my possession," Vincent answered.

"Remarkable," Robert continued to whisper, scrutinizing each angle. Seemingly transfixed, he paid no notice to Vincent's concern. Instead, he inquired, "Do you see this?" causing Martin and Vincent to huddle closer.

Neither seemed to note anything out of the ordinary as Robert traced the impeccable lines of the hilt and pommel with his fingertip.

"It is exactly the absence of what should be," Robert cryptically explained. "Here, along the handle," he continued, tracing the ivory and silver fittings. "There are no signs of wear, no tool marks of any kind. It is as though the blade and its mountings are of one seamless forging."

Martin and Vincent in turn ran their fingers along the blade's contours. It was as Robert had said; there were no gaps nor imperfections where blade met hilt or handle connected to pommel.

"What is this 'strange effect' that you mention?" Robert asked, still not taking his gaze from the sword's craftsmanship.

Martin and Vincent exchanged concerned glances.

"The blade. . . glows," Vincent managed, finding no other way to describe it.

Robert looked up from the sword for the first time. Martin nodded to confirm the odd claim.

"In what way?" Robert pressed, seemingly more out of genuine curiosity than disbelief.

"It gives off a white light, blindingly in some situations," Vincent added.

"Under what conditions?" Robert asked.

"While we were on the ship the pattern of the blade glowed an intense light," Vincent supplied.

Robert seemed deep in thought. He left their immediate presence and began rummaging through several containers on a table on the far side of the tent.

"When did it cease to glow?" he asked while facing away.

Vincent continued, though with growing trepidation, "I'm sure it was just a coincidence, but the glowing seemed to stop when a certain member of the crew from the captured galley . . . vanished."

At this, Robert did seem taken aback. Even though the account bordered on the fantastic, the knowledgeable knight did not discount the captain's words but instead focused his mind toward discovering the source of the mystery. All the while, he did not stop searching through containers and shelves.

"Have you ever heard of such an occurrence?" Martin ventured.

"Oh, I have heard much taller and whimsical tales, though from individuals much more harried and beaten from the crusade," Robert answered, halting his search after producing a parchment.

"What have you found?" Vincent inquired, as he and Martin drew closer.

"This is a very old document," Robert prefaced as he held it out for all to view. "It details part of the tale of Roland."

Vincent and Martin could tell that the writing was nearly illegible and in Latin, but toward the bottom of the tattered and worn paper was a drawing that immediately caught their attention.

"I must come with you," Robert demanded more than requested. "I feel that we are about to witness either an amazing epiphany or a dreadful catastrophe."

Vincent nodded his wordless approval as his eyes took in an unmistakably perfect rendering of the Damascus Sword.

V

Martin and Vincent spent the remainder of the day touring and packing Robert's cache of relics and documents. While Robert did not subscribe to the furor raised over relics of the Holy Land or Christianity, he did find their origins and stories to be fascinating. This was a sentiment to which the Ballecetine knights could certainly attest as many of the ranks of the crusaders not only sought such artifacts but also believed that they held powers of some import.

Throughout the day, Robert related the tale of Roland, a valiant knight who had lived over two hundred years ago. While the details of his exploits had been embellished to be sure, there was no denying the connection of the Damascus Sword to his legacy.

"It was said that Roland wielded the legendary blade, *Durendal*, which was unbreakable," Robert divulged. "Only he, the knight called *Paladin*, was found worthy to use the sword."

Vincent secretly questioned this line of reasoning. If what lay wrapped upon his back truly were the legendary sword of the Paladin, and only those found worthy could wield it, then why had Vincent been allowed to possess the blade after such a cowardly and vile act had been committed by him and his men?

"It was also said that the blade chose its bearer," Robert continued. "And that others who attempted to use it met with great difficulty."

"Does anything in the account speak to the blade glowing?" Vincent asked as the last of the contents of Robert's possessions were emptied from his tent.

"Nothing," Robert admitted.

Martin, Vincent, and Robert stood in silent contemplation for a moment before a familiar voice broke onto the scene.

"Captain!" James shouted from across an expanse. He was carrying the wooden contraption from the war galley that he and William had been crafting to pass the time.

Vincent turned and introduced Robert to William and James.

"We have struck upon something truly revolutionary," William explained. Vincent could not recall seeing the stoic knight excited to such a degree in the short time he had known him.

In response to the lofty assertion, James loaded two crossbow bolts into the grooves of the hefty weapon. The archer knight seemed to have ultimate confidence as he raised the weapon and aimed it toward an innocuous wooden crate. An uneasy silence followed during which time Vincent seemed convinced that the proof of the deed should surely have been evidenced.

William turned inward toward his ally, who contended with the firing mechanism in visible disdain. Finally, the device fired, but the effect was far less than revolutionary, as one bolt shattered upon impacting its own support and the other arced harmlessly into the ground not ten feet from James' stance.

A tense span of several seconds transpired during which no one moved nor spoke. James, who had been startled by the splintering of the arrow and jumped back, held the implement in contempt and seemed for a moment to be considering heaving it to the ground if not for William's quick and decisive intervention. The pair shared a hushed, if heated, exchange which Vincent and the others could not decipher, and then retreated without another word toward the coast and the waiting galley. Robert was the one to break the silence.

"I believe that there is a location of interest to us," he offered.

Vincent and Martin welcomed the redirection.

"A priory that I had often desired to visit before leaving," Robert explained. "Depending on your final destination it may be possible for us to go there and learn more of this relic."

"We sail for Ballecetine," Martin supplied.

"The Priory of Vale lies along the coastal path inland, not a great deflection from your desired route if memory serves," Robert replied, his interest in the growing mystery becoming apparent.

"That is true," Vincent conceded. "If you know this location to hold answers to what we are currently experiencing, then we will make our course directly."

Robert, Martin, and Vincent shared a moment of sublime clarity. As they traversed the distance toward their waiting transport, each took solace in the company of the others. Vincent lagged behind initially, allowing Martin and Robert to go on ahead and engage in conversation. He viewed the crusaders preparing the vessels, loading cargo, and making preparations for the journey home. As was his wont, Vincent observed from a distance and drew conclusions inwardly that directed his words and actions. One thing that he was not, however, was a believer in omens or indirect influences upon his motives. The pragmatic captain of the guard took in the concrete and observable, discarding the abstract and obscure. As he stepped toward the bustling portside activity, however, Vincent resolved to maintain an open mind toward the confusing events unfolding about him.

The morning sun beckoned the renewed group of travelers, and they turned out as one toward the waiting vessels. Having been relieved of their extra passengers, the remaining transports now were habitable to a satisfactory degree for the crusader crews. Vincent, Martin, William, James and the newcomer, Robert, took up their residence upon the pilfered war galley. The fleet set out in true military fashion for the final legs of their journey home toward varied destinations but all sharing the same weary, war-torn spirit.

The Damascus Sword was never more than a few paces away, though fastened securely to the mainmast should its luster or luminosity change for any reason. Robert and Vincent especially were constantly casting their gaze its direction while James and William performed trials and tests upon their new invention. Martin stood aloof for much of the opening hours of the departure, being more interested in leading the vanguard of the procession and avoiding any further complications upon the sea and standing stalwartly upon the swaying prow.

The fleet made excellent time and it was nearing midday when the five knights gathered for the main meal of the day. Robert, being unaccustomed to the routines of the others, at first questioned the wisdom of constructing an open fire upon the deck of a wooden vessel. William assured him of the precautions that had been taken, motioning to the expanse of open sea that could be called to their succor in the event of a conflagration. Robert acquiesced and took a seat among his newfound friends.

"Of course, upon our landing, I shall not ask any of you to continue with Robert and myself toward the Priory of Vale," Vincent led.

Martin was roasting a freshly caught fish while James cast a wounded look and William continued to make adjustments to the contraption.

"Sir," James answered, "I shall accompany you as well."

It did not seem to be a request.

"My lot is, as it always has been, at your side," Martin stated in tone that seemed more matter-of-fact than intended. Upon further reflection, the left-handed knight would understand that his verbal response was not requisite but possibly a result of his need to stake his fealty among present company.

The group's attention then turned toward the toiling inventor and innovator William, who sensed the heat of their collective gazes and looked up absently.

"I would welcome the opportunity," he spoke awkwardly.

With this, the word of those gathered, Vincent was emboldened to memorialize the event. He stood and strode toward the Damascus Sword, released it from its bonds, and rejoined the knights. He held the sword high in his right hand as he spoke.

"Then by your words spoken upon the deck of our stolen vessel, do I declare and establish a new order."

Vincent walked among the four knights, who set aside their current endeavors and each took a knee.

"Sir Robert Breagil," Vincent pronounced, lowering and setting the flat of the blade upon Robert's shoulder. Robert accepted his newfound position with silent profundity and resolve to discover the secrets of the relic resting upon him.

"Sir William Reilu," Vincent spoke, turning to his right and announcing the resourceful knight. William bowed his countenance and closed his eyes to the solemn mood of the moment. He set to use his mind and faculties toward the resolution of the group no matter the cost.

"Sir James Laphrea," Vincent next announced, setting the blade upon the archer knight's prostrate form. James had not before been a part of such an assembly and at once welcomed the responsibility and challenge.

"Sir Martin Cleahim," Vincent declared lastly and set the blade upon his left shoulder. Martin felt a stirring within; there was something occurring on the deck of their vessel now that bespoke events that transcended outer appearances. He could not define the emotion but to know that this was not a mere symbolic act; the weight of the calling was palpable.

Vincent retracted the blade and stood in the midst of them.

"Rise, renewed and resolved. Stand, *Knights of the Damascene Order.*"

VI

A purpose now united the five men on the war galley. Whereas before they were connected by mere happenstance and acquaintance, now there was a focal point and destination always ahead. A few days' journey would land them back upon home soil and the true test would begin. Each knight saw his role as vital toward the greater goal of discovering the meaning of the Damascus Sword and their part in fulfilling a higher purpose.

Several trials of the double crossbow had secured its place as a primary weapon of choice in James' mind, even though each attempt had not earned unquestioned confidence. At the very least, serious injury or damaging setbacks had not delayed the ingenious weapon's development. The archer knight stood upon the prow with his newfound invention as though willing a target worthy of his mettle to present itself.

Martin and Vincent stood at the mainmast while Robert had found a willing participant in the sorting of many volumes of texts and trinkets below in William who, having seemingly mastered the manual element of his expertise, now turned toward sharpening the mental. The late afternoon sun descended ahead, casting longer and longer shadows behind the crew.

James seemed intermittently shifty and tense at one point, and Vincent traversed the deck to join him ahead.

"What is it?" The captain plied.

James pointed off toward the horizon. Vincent strained his vision but could see nothing.

"There," James insisted. "Just below the clouds."

By this time, Martin had joined them, though neither could match the young knight's acuity. "Describe what you see," Martin urged.

"Several spots . . ." James was searching for words.

Martin and Vincent peered ahead, still unseeing. It was at that moment that William emerged from the lower decks and decided to join the congregating group near the front of the vessel.

"What are we watching?" he asked.

There was no immediate answer, but momentarily Martin stepped forward and also pointed skyward. Vincent and William, almost as one, saw what the others viewed and attempted to make sense of what their eyes were telling them.

Now, very clearly in the waning light of day, several dots coalesced into form. A flock of birds became visible, though their approach harbored ominous feelings of ill-will. Vincent could not immediately identify the source of his paranoia, but looking about to the other knights he could tell that he was not the only one experiencing the effect.

"What are they?" William gasped, walking toward the front of the ship as though a few more feet of perspective would enlighten him further.

Vincent had no answer, but as he turned to contemplate the situation he noticed an odd shadow casting itself upon the deck.

It was the Damascus Sword.

"Martin," Vincent spoke, not taking his eyes from the luminescent blade still affixed to the mainmast, "alert the other transports to prepare for battlestations."

At this, the other knights on deck took action. Each witnessed the intensifying glow of the mysterious sword as a portent of danger; whatever was coming toward them, it bore only animosity. Martin signaled to the trailing vessels to prepare ranged weaponry and James felt his blood boil, raising the magnificent double crossbow, armed with two bolts and a healthy supply in reserve.

Vincent felt that he must release the Damascus Sword from its restraints. It was shining an increasingly bright cadence of light and again imparted a cool, though not painfully cold, sensation as he held it aloft once more. William and Martin took up longbows and Robert ascended to the deck, having heard and sensed the increased activity above. Martin handed him a longbow, which he accepted without question and joined the others toward middeck.

There were roughly fifteen approaching targets, James surmised as he took aim at the lead representative and fired. A disappointing creak, followed by a splintering crack filled the air as the bolt that had been loaded into the upper track misfired and jammed under tension. James cursed audibly and cast the weapon aside. William had thankfully thought to equip the galley with longbows enough for all.

"They are birds of prey," James shouted as he took a bow and an arrow.

"They are coming directly for our position," Martin added, notching an arrow upon his string.

Vincent initially made to take up a bow himself, but felt that he should not leave the Damascus Sword unattended. It was glowing a pulsating rhythm much like before in the presence of the old man. Though not nearly as intense, it was growing in magnitude as the birds approached.

"Eagles," William supplied, as he saw that four archers stood ready.

"Wait," Martin commanded, holding steady.

James had the best eyes of the group and could begin to make out the finer details of the swarming flock. They were certainly eagles, as William had identified, but they were proportionally much larger and more muscular than any the archer knight had ever seen. He inwardly doubted that their current ranged weaponry would have much effect upon them.

"Fire!" Martin shouted and four arrows flew. True to aim, all four struck targets. Two struck the lead eagle, which fell. Two others were hit as well but continued the offensive.

"Fire at will!" Martin added.

After the war galley's first volley, the trailing transports understood the tactic and flights of arrows launched alternately from behind Vincent's ship, reaping similar results. It was unavoidable that a sizable remnant of the group of attackers was to light upon them, for what purpose none could surmise until they dove as bolts of lightning upon their target: the bearer of the Damascus Sword. Even James' rapid rate of fire could not divert the smaller group and, as they descended at blinding speed, further attempts to intercept them with mere human reflexes and aim fell sorely ineffective. The Damascus Sword grew in brightness the closer the birds of prey flew. The galley crew abandoned long-range attacks and drew swords for the final clash

Enormous wingspans blocked the sun and oversized talons gripped onto the deck. William and Martin quickly fell upon the first intruders to land, effectively dispatching them as more landed and took their places. These last attackers took to landing upon the crusaders' shoulders and began furiously tearing and slashing with their hooked beaks.

Three eagles remained aloft, circling the vessel, centering upon Vincent. It seemed the others were a distraction, as the four knights in the party were now separated, and at the precise moment that all their backs were turned, the crafty birds spiraled downward. The Damascus Sword flew, bisecting one foe, but two struck true and knocked Vincent to the deck. The eagles cared little for inflicting damage upon the prone captain but clawed and fought for the glowing sword still in his tight grasp.

The four knights spun and made to intercept the melee, but it was too late. One of the ferocious eagles had clawed a bloody scene in wresting the sword from Vincent's grip while the other took flight with the blade's silver pommel firmly in a closed talon and escaped toward the reddening sunset. James took aim with the nearest longbow and impaled the offending bird squarely through the abdomen. As it died, falling and losing its grip on the Damascus Sword, its partner deftly swooped downward and retrieved the weapon before it could fall into the sea.

"Shoot it down!" Martin ordered, as by now the surrounding transports had witnessed the situation. The volume and frequency of missiles fired from the ally vessels did not match the archer knight's accuracy or efficiency to any degree, but it was their sheer number that saw the pilfering eagle eventually succumb to several indirect blows and fall into the water. The Damascus Sword also fell and immediately sank. As the galley crew stood in momentary shock regarding who should go in to find the sword before it became irretrievable, Vincent leaped from a running start and dove into the cold water leaving trails of blood in his wake.

The Damascus Sword had entirely lost its luminescence, which made it increasingly difficult to track as it knifed downward at a great rate of speed. Vincent did not know the extent of his injuries but pushed himself to dive ever faster and lower, forcing his lungs to endure however long it took to save the plunging sword. The sting of the water across open wounds and slashes caused him to lose his concentration for a moment and close his eyes but his body continued to dive and in a stroke of blind luck he reached out and gripped the cold silver pommel. As he did, a sensation similar to that when he had fallen into the water and retrieved the sword earlier in the journey overtook him and he felt himself slipping from consciousness.

Can you hear me?

Vincent registered the sound, but could not feel his body. He felt as though he were in a state between reality and dream, the voice being the only anchor of familiarity. It was the unknown figure from the other vision-like occurrences. Vincent found that he could not will his voice to answer and then concluded that he did not have a corporeal presence in this iteration of the other-world.

You can communicate with me by your thoughts.

"Who are you?" Vincent thought.

I am what you will discover.

"That is not an answer," Vincent retorted in what he hoped was a more stern tone of thought.

After this, there was a brief pause.

"Why was I chosen to bear the sword?" Vincent continued, sensing that, as the other visions had, this one was coming to its close rapidly.

You will know sooner than you realize.

Vincent's next waking memory was of being propelled toward the surface much faster than he was capable of swimming. It was fortuitous, as he emerged just as his lungs could take no more. Damascus Sword in hand, the captain pulled himself aboard the low-sided galley to assess his injuries and ponder the things he had seen and heard.

At first, Vincent could not ascertain the wide-eyed and speechless stares of the galley crew. He knew that he had possibly acted rashly in diving into the sea without warning, but it was hardly an uncharacteristic deed or ill-advised considering the circumstances.

44

Then, just as he was able to collect his thoughts, he experienced what the others were witnessing.

Deep gashes and scratches on his forearms and face knitted themselves closed before the eyes of all. After a moment, the only evidence that there had been blood shed was the stain upon his clothing. The transformation spanned a mere ten or fifteen seconds, during which time the captain felt power flowing through him from the Damascus Sword. He did not feel the penetrating cold sensation but instead another equally powerful transmission entered him. Holding the blade at eye level, Vincent could not quantify or analyze the experience. For one of the only times he could remember, the Captain of the Guard of Ballecetine felt a wanton abandonment of his pragmatic senses and enjoyed a simple and inexplicable wave of transcendent euphoria.

VII

Robert was the first to broach Vincent's personal space. The inquisitive knight reached out and touched the places where deep wounds once covered the captain's arms. In equal bewilderment, Vincent looked on with stunned expression as the other three approached.

"While the Damascus Sword is in my possession, I feel a growing power from within," Vincent explained. He purposely did not yet reveal the odd visions he had been receiving, deciding that he needed to discover their meaning for himself before involving others.

Robert nodded in approval as Vincent spoke. "This is to be expected," he added cryptically, to the confused stares of the others. "It was also said that when the *Paladin* wielded *Durendal* he was virtually invincible to physical pain or injury."

"The sword has lost its light," Martin remarked.

"This is the greatest curiosity," Robert continued. "I do not recall any account of the Paladin's blade glowing. Perhaps the scribes at the Priory of Vale will be able to give us clarity upon this effect."

Vincent and the others seemed content at this explanation. From that time onward, he did not allow the Damascus Sword to leave his person, instead wrapping it in a thick cloth and carrying it upon his back, slung over his right shoulder should its light alert them to other impending dangers.

The remainder of the seabound journey, thankfully, elapsed without further incident. It happened that the fleet made landfall on the shores of England in early morning, which facilitated the crews to disperse and fall out into their ranks toward home. Vincent personally saw the various detachments off until only the Ballecetine contingent remained with the exception of Robert, William and James.

"Sir Stipe," Vincent called into the gathered knights.

"Captain," came a reply from within, followed by the emergence of a knight who stood a head taller than the rest.

"I am placing you in command of the return journey to Ballecetine," Vincent continued, looking up to meet the eyes of the man to whom he was entrusting the care of his men.

"Yes, sir," Sir Stipe answered without question.

"Send my regards to Lord West, and Diana," he added. "We will return as soon as it is possible."

Sir Stipe left expediently and within a few moments only five knights stood against the landscape. Vincent and Martin watched their brethren depart, wishing to be among them to walk through Ballecetine's gates but knowing that more pressing matters called them forth.

The *Damascene Order* was able to procure horses and supplies easily enough, even a small cart to transport supplies including Robert's extensive documentation and research. They rode in rehearsed formation; Robert at the point with the supplies cart, William and James in the middle with Vincent and Martin riding at the rear. The wily captain relished and sought this most advantageous point from whence to keep the pace of the group and also react to any threat with all his assets in plain view. He also rode on Martin's right-hand side to allow both to play to their strengths if the group were to be flanked from either direction.

The five rode for several hours in near solitude, passing only sporadic commerce as they skirted locally known principalities. The sun was nearing the horizon as Robert slowed the procession and pulled to the side. Vincent and Martin rode up beside as the group conferred.

"The Priory is near, just over these hills ahead," Robert explained, pointing toward the horizon. Vincent estimated they would reach their destination just before dusk. He also knew enough of local geography to know that the Ballecetine knights by now would be making their report to Lord West. Their oblique route was carrying them no closer or farther from home and, at the very least, Vincent surmised they would be setting foot upon home soil by this time tomorrow.

"Captain," William called from behind.

Turning to face James and William, Vincent exposed Martin and Robert to the source of William's attention. The Damascus Sword was emitting a faint ray of light from beneath its covering. Vincent immediately swung the securing strap off his shoulder and slid the blade from its protective sheath. Though not nearly as luminescent as previous encounters, its light was definitely growing in intensity.

This in itself caused the party to arm for combat. James raised the fearsome double crossbow, fresh from a newly-calibrated tension and diagnostic approval from the architect William, in anticipation of another encounter with avian opponents. Martin drew his hand-and-a-half which suited his arm strength well while mounted. Robert and William brandished battleswords but kept the longbows on the supply cart in the center of their formation. Vincent rode into the forefront *Damascene* in hand and prodded his steed to a slow walk, sensing the effect to strengthen as he moved.

As they crested the first small hill along the road toward the Priory of Vale, Vincent stopped abruptly, causing the rest of the party to flank him and leave the path slightly to view the landscape ahead and below. From this higher ground, the outer buildings of the Priory proper were visible, but that was not the reason that Vincent had halted his progress. A single, horse-mounted figure stood in opposition at a point roughly halfway between them and their goal. From the rider's posture Vincent knew immediately who it was, stationary and facing them as though to issue a challenge. It was the old man from the war galley, verified by the intensifying glow from the blade in the captain's grasp.

The enigmatic old man did not retreat or attempt to escape as the party of crusaders rode to intercept him with weapons drawn. As the knights encircled him in a visually unnecessary display of might, he only smiled a gapped grin and cast his gaze unwaveringly upon Vincent.

"You have found me, my son," he spoke with a pronounced cackle, which was difficult to identify as purposeful or the result of ill health. Vincent noted a decline in his physical attributes and a marked sense of frailty that had not been present the first time they had met.

"Explain the purpose of your escaping the ship," Vincent pressed, ignoring the claim to his kinship.

"You mean," he spat, coughing profusely and nearly falling from his steed, "my disappearance."

"What is your connection to the Damascus Sword?" Vincent demanded, sensing that there may be precious little time left for him to interrogate his subject, either from supernatural vanishing or mere decaying mortality.

"You do not understand. . ." a round of debilitating wheezing and hacking cut his answer short. Vincent made to catch him as his balance faltered and he fell backward from his saddle but no reaction or reflex could move fast enough as the old man again disappeared just as his body hit the ground, leaving behind only a solitary horse with no provisions or indications as to his identity.

"This is becoming very peculiar," Robert commented, never taking his eyes from the Damascus Sword, which lost its shine the instant the old man disappeared.

"There is an uncanny connection between this blade and the old man," Vincent was thinking out loud.

"He called you his son," James added.

Vincent nodded. "That is not lost upon me."

A few silent moments passed, during which time the attention of each was slowly drawn back toward the Priory. Vincent strode to the forefront of the assembly and spoke.

"I feel that we should learn much very soon," he spoke gravely, casting his attention to each of the knights in turn. "It may be some time before we see our homes again. If any now doubt the calling, renounce and resume your lives in your home province but do not cast your lot among us half-heartedly."

None spoke. All stood stalwartly in unity.

"No man will renounce the call," Martin concluded.

Vincent nodded. As one, the *Damascene Order* took the trail ahead toward the resolution of the oddities that had befallen the homeward bound crusaders.

VIII

Stables and outbuildings dotted the perimeter of the Priory, all of which unattended. For this leg of the journey, Vincent took the forefront while James brought up the rear, the mercurial double crossbow loaded and ready for a preemptive strike if necessary. Martin, William and Robert trod carefully in the center of the formation, eyes wary in all directions and upward to the skies.

The central structure of the compound was a keep-like building encircled by gardens and a gated wall that served a more aesthetic than defensive function. Vincent and the party dismounted and tethered their horses at an empty stable, stashing the cart as well beneath its vacant roof.

Robert and William equipped lightly, each taking only a light battlesword. James armed himself with a light sidearm but endeavored to redeem the double crossbow and carried it, still loaded with two bolts, as his ranged weapon. It was a testament to his faith in his ally's recent adjustments that the consummate archer chose not to wield a more reliable longbow, which he concluded would become more of a liability than an asset in close quarters.

Vincent unsheathed the Damascus Sword from its crude covering, knowing that due to the simple length of the weapon he would likely be required to carry it in hand for the duration of this encounter for lack of a suitable scabbard. This he deemed a blessing and a curse, as having constant scrutiny of the blade's status would alert himself and the party of danger but its size might prove a detriment in enclosed confines. The captain considered carefully and chose to carry the Damascus Sword exclusively with no encumbering additions to his arsenal.

Martin, the consummate swordsman of Ballecetine, took a divergent approach. The trusted hand-and-a-half was always on his right hip, but a more suitable battlesword found its place in his hand with a various multitude of weaponry hidden upon his person. He was also the only knight to encumber himself with full mail; the others had shed such hindrances at the port in favor of comfort.

Vincent led the group toward the front gate. Upon reaching the perimeter of the keep, he tested the defenses and found that the mechanism was locked. There were no immediately visible means of summoning anyone to assist them, so a slight glance toward the resourceful William produced a solution in moments. The gate swung open, Damascus Sword leading the party inward.

Now the undefended inner citadel stood before them. Holding the sword up to eye level, Vincent approached the large double wooden doors that separated the courtyard from the keep and, casting a gaze of finality toward the party, tried the handle. Just as his hand lighted upon it, a voice called from above.

"Knights of the Cross, identify yourself!"

The party leaped back, James training the crossbow upward out of pure reflex. Three longbowmen stood upon the upper level of the citadel, ensconced between strategic battlements, all with arrows at the ready and trained upon the intruding party. Vincent took a step back to better survey the threat and explain themselves. A fourth, unarmed figure, held out his arm and at this gesture the longbowmen stepped down.

"We are returning knights from the Crusade," Vincent answered.

This interested the unarmed man above, though Vincent could tell that it was not his words that had produced their safety but the sight of the Damascus Sword.

"To what lord to you swear allegiance?"

Vincent looked hesitantly about the group.

"We are the *Damascene Order*," he improvised, playing both his questioner's curiosity and his disinterest in explaining the party's varying loyalties.

At this, the fourth figure retreated behind the wall, along with the three longbowmen. Vincent and the knights stepped back from the doorway in anticipation of a face-to-face meeting with the inhabitants of the Priory. After a brief pause, the figure from above opened the imposing doors, motioning the party to enter.

"My name is Christopher Alexander," he introduced. He and his attending guards wore plain brown clothing and an air of austerity overtook the knights as they treaded into Christopher's domain.

Vincent took the forefront, holding the Damascus Sword low as he introduced the party to their hosts. Christopher nodded in respect as each knight stepped forward though it was, as always, the sword that garnered the attention of all in the keep. After the introductions were completed, Vincent and Robert stepped forward to explain the purpose of their visit, though their profoundly deliberate host chose to fill the gap before the knights could elaborate.

"You have come in search of information related to the Paladin," he explained.

"We knew this location to be of some import regarding the legends, especially of the blade *Durendal*," Robert expounded.

Christopher nodded knowingly as Robert spoke, eyes fixed upon the blade.

"Do you believe this blade to be the legendary weapon of the Paladin?" Christopher inquired.

"We do," Robert offered, "and what is more, we have witnessed a curious effect that seems to further the mystery surrounding its power."

At this, Christopher looked up from the blade for the first time. He waved his attendants off and approached closer. Vincent motioned to hold the blade upward to their host's scrutiny, but Christopher initially shrank from the gesture, raising his hands to indicate he did not wish to touch the sword.

"The surface of the blade glows in certain situations," Robert added.

Christopher seemed unconcerned at this new revelation but only bent closer to view the swirls and patterns of the impeccable alloy inches from his eyes. After several silent moments, the host straightened his posture and stepped back from the party.

"I believe that we may be able to help you find the answers that you seek," he spoke after a heavy pause. "It will take some time."

"Sir Robert is an expert in antiquities and relics," Vincent supplied. "Perhaps he can be of some assistance."

"I have brought documents and relics from the Holy Land that may be of some help as well," Robert offered.

"That may be important indeed," Christopher concurred.

Vincent remained with Christopher as the majority of the *Damascene Order* exited to retrieve Robert's trove. This left the captain and host alone and as the door closed after his men, Vincent lost no time in his planned interrogation.

"Why am only I able to wield the sword when it glows?" he asked in hasty tone that came across more harshly than intended.

"The blade has chosen you, Vincent," the attendant answered in anticipation of the query. "One thing you must understand about the blade is that the longer you possess it the more connected you will become to it."

Christopher seemed to share Vincent's desire to converse confidentially and inject as much content into their time together as possible.

"I have . . . visions when the blade glows," Vincent added.

Christopher took this information in stride as well as Robert's exposition regarding the blade's glowing properties, though he did seem to fall into thought for a few moments before answering Vincent's admission. "The visions will begin to make more sense with time. The blade remembers its past owners and each of those valiant bearers is imprinted upon the sword. The experiences and even thoughts and emotions of those who have come before you may well surface given enough time."

Vincent looked down at the weapon with newfound clarity. He was not losing his mind. The curious captain was about to launch a new offensive of questions when a heavy pounding from the main doors interrupted them. Vincent's instincts rose within him, and Christopher's unspoken trepidation preceded his men's hasty reappearance onto the scene at the same time as the pounding upon the front door took on a battering quality.

Vincent instinctively looked to the Damascus Sword. Its color and brightness were normal. Whatever entity stood outside with increasing desire to enter was not a trigger for the sword's alert mechanism and, ostensibly, his visions.

"Sir," reported one of the longbowmen. "A dozen knights from Redmont approach, demanding entrance."

"Redmont?" Vincent whispered.

Christopher was unshaken. He wordlessly accompanied the guards to the upper level to address the hostile party while Vincent stood by idly, contemplating his next course of action. His men were, with any luck, absent from the immediate scene though he could not anticipate their actions upon discovering what had transpired.

There were no windows within sight from which Vincent could survey the situation. The pounding had subsided for the time being, and voices could be heard but not comprehended clearly from his location. The captain made to attempt exit from another avenue and ran from the entry foyer toward the flank of the keep. After a few twists and turns, he found an unsecured egress. Warily opening the door, which was far less obtrusive and prominent than the large central portal, Vincent peered around the edge and saw the open expanse of countryside before him. Gaining his bearings quickly, the captain spotted the roofs of the stables and outbuildings ahead, though he doubted that he could make for them without being seen by those occupying the main entrance. He only hoped that his men had been as observant and had not accidentally stumbled upon the situation.

In this moment of indecision, while Vincent strained his hearing to ascertain something as to the goings-on at the main doors, and object struck his right shoulder, causing him to spin about. A pebble rolled away harmlessly and the captain looked up to see the rest of the *Order* holding a defensive position upon the roof of the keep. A moment of intense relief was followed by bewilderment as Vincent could find no immediate means of ascending to their position and did not dare shout upward to inquire further.

Presently, rope followed pebble, and Vincent climbed upward, launching himself from ledge to frame in a hurried display of prowess that saw him reunited with the others in moments.

"What news?" Vincent asked as the group trod carefully toward the front of the keep.

"We witnessed a detachment of Redmont knights on approach as we reached the stables," Martin reported. "They had not seen us, so we circled toward the back and scaled the keep to get a better look."

54

"What is Redmont doing here?" Vincent spat, forgetting for the moment that only himself and Martin would have any frame of reference for the history of conflict between the aforementioned principality and their native Ballecetine.

"I could not say," Martin answered as they came to the forefront and crouched low.

From here, the group could look out and see that the Redmont contingent remained outside the walls of the keep, and Christopher was arguing vehemently against their insistent entrance into the proper. For what purpose the aggressors sought admittance could not be discovered from their position, but there had been far too many odd occurrences and anomalies for the Captain of the Guard and bearer of *Damascene* to tolerate in the return home to this point. At that moment Vincent made the determination to take an active role in the events that were unfolding and one glance to the faces of his men confirmed this growing sentiment among the *Order*. It was time to begin constructing meaning from the chaos mounting around them. It was time to take initiative instead of allowing events to swirl around them.

It was time to act.

IX

Christopher's patience and stalling had reached their end. He retreated into the Priory, alerting his men to prepare for what was most assuredly to be a full assault.

"What do they want?" Vincent asked as he and his men availed themselves for the cause.

"It is very strange, very strange indeed," Christopher repeated himself. "They demand to see the Tapestry."

The weight with which their host pronounced the item of interest diverted Vincent's attention. Any further exposition on the matter was to be saved for a later time, however, as the punctuating blows being dealt to the Priory's main doors called all hands to action.

"Station your archers above, and wait for our signal," Vincent urged. "James, you accompany them on the rooftop," he added.

Christopher nodded and his men left hastily with the crossbow archer not far behind.

"Where is the nearest side exit?" Vincent inquired.

"This way," Christopher answered, leading them away from the growing clamor of the main entrance.

As they left the building, the constant battering ceased and an odd silence followed. Christopher brought the party outside to the weakening light of evening and all halted in tense anticipation; as long as the Redmont knights were employed in their attempted entrance they could be tracked, but now Vincent and the others crept along the perimeter of the inner wall toward the corner in uncertainty.

Damascus Sword in hand, Vincent edged outward with just enough perspective to glimpse the front of the citadel and dodged back again.

"They seem to be preparing to leave," Vincent divulged to the group in hushed tones.

"They might be a scouting party meant to gauge the Priory's defenses," William offered.

Martin visibly concurred with this sentiment. "Then we have only two choices available," he concluded. "Either we prepare the Priory for an assault soon, or we make sure the scouting party does not reach the main contingent."

"In any case, these men know what they are looking for, and where to find it," Vincent surmised.

"Then we have little choice," Christopher added.

Vincent seemed to have made a decision and took an initial step into the open when a faint light from his side caused all in the party to momentarily freeze.

It was the Damascus Sword, emitting a faint, but growing, luminescence from within.

The captain had no way to immediately hide the sword's light and at the current stage of the evening its presence would be a beacon ruining any effort at gaining the advantage through surprise.

"Shall we alert the archers to open fire?" Martin suggested, endeavoring to salvage the situation alertly.

"Wait," Vincent called, holding the blade low and behind as he peered around the edge of the wall again. He observed the group that had approached halt in the advance of another figure. Out on the open path, Vincent recognized the form at once. It was Lord Gallock of Redmont himself, conversing with his men who had formed a semicircle before him.

"Lord Gallock is here," Vincent reported, then looked out over the horizon in the direction he had come. There was a faint glow of firelight rising from the land, as from a battalion making camp for the night. "And I believe preparing the Priory for an assault may be futile at this point as it appears a rather large detachment of men are making camp just over the hills."

The group pondered this news for a moment. In Martin's and Vincent's minds, the same conclusion had been reached. If Lord Gallock had penetrated this far toward Ballecetine, there was no telling what devastation had been wrought upon the land and nearby towns. Ballecetine Manor was not so distant as to be unassailable; where were the ranks of their native land? Had Ballecetine already fallen?

What of Lord West, and Diana?

"Captain," Martin broke the silence, "I believe that we must in good faith attempt reconnaissance of the larger group."

"Definitely so," Vincent concurred. "We will wait until it becomes a bit darker and form our party."

The group watched as the Redmont contingent, led by their lord, disappeared over the hills toward the growing light of the enemy campfires. As they did so, Vincent observed the Damascus Sword's brightness diminish and ultimately fade to natural.

A small group from among the thirteen currently inhabiting the priory was chosen. James, William and Martin would steal into the night while the rest would bolster defenses. Initially a messenger was to have been sent to Ballecetine to ascertain its fate and readiness but every member of the group was determined vital to the current dilemma. Additionally, with the uncertainty of the political atmosphere in their immediate vicinity, caution was the rule when considering sorties into the countryside.

Vincent acquiesced to the group's petition to have him remain behind as his presence with the Damascus Sword and its unknown properties might compromise the stealth of the party. He and the larger group secured the citadel's perimeter and made an ample supply of arrows and longbows accessible from every point of advance. If a full assault were the order given by Lord Gallock, they would need to soften the lines as quickly as possible without risking hand to hand combat at such uneven odds.

In that vein, vigil was kept as the night wore on. None would sleep but in short, tense naps with a weapon within immediate reach. Vincent looked to the clear sky and the full moon above. The pale light reflected from the tempestuous pattern of lines across the Damascus Sword's fearsome edges. Many had given their lives in the campaign abroad and it was possible that some who had risked much for a foreign escapade would do so only to lose their lives on home soil. The Captain of the Guard stared deeply into the wavy pattern of the blade's steel which mirrored his uncertainties and hopeful visages of those he cared for most.

Martin led the trio in a circuitous path and avoided the main road toward the enemy camp. As expected, the light and accompanying clamor of a large mass of soldiers grew as they approached. Finding cover in a small copse of trees, the three crouched down and learned what they could.

The soldiers were in a basin through which a river ran that Martin knew to connect to tributaries very near home. Knowing his local geography, he surmised that a group the size before them would surely have been noticed and hopefully engaged as it passed through the heart of Ballecetine. This engendered his concern and dulled his hope at the possibility of an intact Ballecetine Manor in its wake.

"About fifty mounted knights and another two hundred men at arms?" William estimated.

James nodded gravely. "It is hard to tell how many archers are among them. That will determine how best to defend the Priory."

Martin remained silent, deep in thought.

"What is your assessment of the situation?" William posited in his direction.

Waiting another moment until he had formulated his concern, Martin replied, "I cannot help but think that even this force is a satellite of a larger invasion group. This number of men would not be adequate to venture so far from home soil. There must be a central camp nearby . . ."

As Martin trailed off, James and William turned their attention upward and toward the mass before them.

"There do seem to be various roads leading to and from the camp," James added.

Martin was wandering away absently, visualizing the surrounding countryside. "There is a village not so far from here that might have the resources to sustain a larger force in the field," he uttered partially to himself.

"Is there a history of conflict between your land and Redmont?" William asked.

Martin nodded vaguely in the negative. "There have been skirmishes, but nothing approaching outright hostility to this degree. It is puzzling what has set events in motion at this time."

The three stood in a plaintive mood, each thinking of what should be the next course of action when motion along the perimeter of the enemy camp beckoned their attention.

"There," Martin pointed. "What is that?"

James stepped forward and focused upon a group of individuals congregating at the edge of camp facing their location.

"They seem to be forming a circle for some purpose," he answered in puzzled tone.

There, before their eyes, ten knights of Redmont formed a ring a number of paces distant from the group. Lord Gallock followed them and stood in the center of the ring. He seemed to be speaking to his men, but after closer inspection James concluded that he was speaking downward toward the ground. What occurred next caused Martin, James and William to step back and hide again in the stand of trees for cover.

Lord Gallock paced the perimeter of his ring of knights and just as he concluded one complete revolution, the ground at the center of the ring began to undulate and swirl. The vegetation was swallowed up in a vortex as three magnificently formed and immediately familiar birds of prey emerged from the maelstrom. They took flight and headed toward the Priory.

Vincent, Robert and Christopher stood atop the citadel in a position advantageous for seeing the scouting party's return as soon as they crested the horizon. The Damascus Sword was propped in a corner battlement visible at once if its status changed in the slightest.

"What is the nature of this tapestry that the men of Redmont seek?" Vincent inquired as the three looked out.

Christopher turned toward the captain and answered. "It is a relic carried back from a previous venture to the Holy Land."

Robert took notice of the conversation at once, wholly engrossed in its explanation.

"It was called the *Tapestry of the Immortals* and was said to depict the forces of good and evil in their striving to control mankind."

"And it is kept here?" Robert interjected.

"Yes," Christopher nodded. "In a cavern beneath the Priory's foundation several valuable artifacts are kept. I myself have only laid eyes upon the object once."

The three stood in silence for a moment.

"What value could such a relic have to Lord Gallock?" Robert asked.

"It is hard to say," Christopher replied. "No one has expressed interest in it during my time here."

It appeared as though Vincent was about to add something to the conversation, but activity upon the dark landscape attracted their full attention.

"What is that?" Robert gasped, looking toward the sky.

Vincent knew instantly, and the intensifying light thrown from the Damascus Sword attested to the re-emergence of the feared birds of prey that had attempted to capture the sword previously.

"We have encountered these eagles before," Vincent explained to a confused Christopher. "They seemed to seek the Damascus Sword and nearly made off with it."

Luckily there were only three of them, but their magnificent wingspans made them seem much more menacing than their number would indicate. Vincent retrieved the blade, feeling its coolness become more and more pronounced as the finer features of the looming enemies became visible. No verbal order was necessary at this point; Vincent laid the sword down carefully at his feet and the three lookouts took up longbows and trained them ahead. The moon's glow was their only ally as they released their arrows simultaneously.

One bird was hit and began to fall while the remaining two rose in altitude in preparation for a diving strike while the archers reloaded. By now the Damascus Sword was at full intensity, as bright as Vincent had even seen it glow.

It became increasingly hard to aim as the eagles began their descent. Three missiles flew but none landed true and Vincent, Christopher and Robert ducked behind a battlement for cover as the pair screamed just over their heads and rounded the corner of the citadel for another pass.

Just as they disappeared momentarily, a small party of Christopher's men appeared on the scene after witnessing the commotion. Before anyone could warn them or issue an order, the ravenous birds emerged from the opposite side of the keep and each grasped one of the newcomers firmly with its massive talons and carried off an ally.

Robert and Christopher had armed their longbows again by this point but held fire. The agonized screams of Christopher's men punctuated the cold night air as talons impaled flesh and tore through muscle. The unearthly creatures carried them higher and higher with no effort. After a few moments, they loosened their grip, sending two valuable members of an already divided party to a terrifying and sickening end upon the hard earth below.

Both Christopher and Robert released their arrows at this point, more out of frustration than effectiveness, and each missed significantly as the pair turned and headed back toward the Priory for another onslaught.

Having sustained the loss of two, the party standing atop the citadel now numbered five. Vincent took up the blinding Damascus Sword, while the other four took aim with opportunity for one final strike. This encounter was different, Vincent noted, in that the eagles seemed to be learning. Their single-minded pursuit of the Damascus Sword made them easier to predict the first time; now they were systematically attacking individuals who barred their progress more effectively.

Vincent stood behind the line as four arrows flew, and one target was struck multiple times and fell. The final attacking eagle tore into their line and sent Christopher and Robert to the floor. One of Christopher's remaining allies drew his sidearm to engage the enemy but was too slow and the hooked beak of the massive bird of prey gashed into his neck, crumpling him instantly. A supernatural quickness accompanied the inhuman strength and size of these beasts as neither Vincent nor the last remaining man at his side was able to react fast enough to obstruct the eagle's rapid ascent back into the darkened heavens.

The eagle turned to make a blind-side assault from around the far side of the citadel again. Christopher and Robert rushed to the side of the badly mangled man. This left Vincent, and one final remaining ally to anticipate from whence the next attack would come.

The Damascus Sword was blindingly brilliant at this point as Vincent raised it high in an attempt to cut off the final strike. He and the others waited in tense silence but the attack never came. After a few moments, the remaining party members looked up and saw the eagle perched atop the highest ledge of the priory keep. It seemed to be observing them, but only superficially and had its primary attention diverted to the far horizon.

This directed the incomplete party to cast their gaze distant. Vincent understood then why the Damascus Sword had shone increasingly brighter in the last few moments for, cresting the dark horizon as he stared unbelievingly, a new wave of powerful birds of prey blocked out the weak moonlight on their fevered pace for the bearer of the Damascus Sword.

X

Martin, James and William were hidden when the next group of eagles took flight. This time they counted ten and Martin wondered if that was a good or bad omen. He knew their destination to be the Priory and the retrieval of the Damascus Sword from earlier experience, but the fact that more had been summoned caused him pause.

"We cannot simply stay here and do nothing," James offered.

"That is true," Martin agreed. "We must risk exposing ourselves to help the others. They are no doubt fighting off the eagles as we speak."

James checked the tension and settings on his double crossbow one last time and the three crept out into the darkness. If there were one positive to be taken from their expedition it was that they had succeeded in staying concealed and learning much about the origins of the massive eagles, even if Lord Gallock's connection to them seemed unclear. Martin pondered this as the group made haste to aid their harried allies.

"Perhaps we should take cover in the keep," Christopher suggested after concluding that the man who had been attacked was dead.

Vincent estimated there to be nearly a dozen eagles in this next force and did not relish the thought of fighting them off at such odds. "We are only seven strong after sending out the others and losing three," he thought out loud. As he mused, they made their way toward the entrance and began to filter inside and downward for refuge. Vincent initially followed them toward the exit, but then the Damascus Sword's cold texture and empowering spirit came upon him and he closed the door behind his allies and turned to face the rapidly approaching eagles alone.

As their range tightened, Vincent's grip on the ivory handle relaxed and the weapon became an extension of his arm as he swung downward in time with the initial eagle's point of attack and cleft its form cleanly in half. A second followed immediately on his upstroke and a third as he ducked low, slicing swiftly as he rolled to the floor behind a battlement.

The remnant of the group split to encircle the keep and gather for another pass. Vincent took this opportunity to regain his footing and raised the blade high again, noticing that the blood dissipated and evaporated from its surface to restore its characteristic glow.

A group of four emerged from behind, the leader of which struck true while Vincent spun, knocking him to the floor. The subsequent attackers descended to land upon the prone captain but the blade flew again and two were wounded sufficiently to call off the assault.

Vincent rose and slid with his back to the outer wall to avoid another surprise attack from behind. Looking upward in the dim moonlight he could see their forms circling the keep at a healthy distance, as though formulating the next strategy.

Then, inexplicably, one of their numbers fell from the sky and landed heavily not five feet from his position, having been impaled by two crossbow bolts. Vincent instinctively spun to view the scouting party below, and James loading two more bolts in the redeemed double crossbow.

Quickly focusing his attention above again, Vincent set upon a new tactic. While the circling eagles hesitated, he set the sword down and picked up one of the discarded longbows, firing as rapidly as he could toward the shapes above. Between his efforts, and James' accuracy from below, three more beasts fell before they could muster a new strategy and, predictably, the remaining eagles retreated after suffering losses to more than half their number.

Vincent set the longbow down and examined the carcass of the fallen eagle. Each of its talons was easily as long as his entire hand. What confounded him, as the Damascus Sword predictably lost its luster with their retreat, was their origin and connection to the blade.

Christopher and the remaining population of the Priory soon joined Vincent on the upper level after allowing Martin, William and James entry. There were many tasks at hand such as burying fallen allies and planning a strategy moving forward, which Vincent urged the group to discuss in the great hall where they had first congregated.

"What were you able to learn in your short time away?" Vincent posed toward the prodigal trio.

"We saw Lord Gallock summoning the eagles that attacked you," Martin supplied, leading with what he felt to be the most urgent of news. "There is a group of perhaps two hundred men gathered beyond the hills but possibly more nearby."

This information both answered and posed questions in Vincent's mind.

"So Lord Gallock is in control of the great eagles," Christopher mused.

"What do you know of these eagles?" Vincent posed.

"Only that they are a representation of the supernatural powers that are seeking you out," he supplied. "Perhaps it is time for you to see the object of Lord Gallock's desire."

With this, Christopher led the group to a stairway hidden in the far wall of the keep. It led downward in a sharp circular fashion such that each man had to walk single-file and even then shoulders and knees scraped the edges of the roughly-hewn stone.

Torches lined the outer circumference of the walls, and they seemed to have been recently lit. No doubt, Vincent surmised, when Redmont's soldiers arrived on the scene the relics below had been secured and checked.

Eventually the stairway leveled off and became a short corridor that terminated in a sturdy iron door. The corridor was not of sufficient length for the entire group to occupy, so several of those who trailed behind remained in the staircase while Christopher produced a large key and opened the door.

Vincent was the first after Christopher to cross the threshold. What greeted them was an expansive space that seemed to have been carved out of the bedrock itself. Their point of entry was at the top of its height and widening stone-carved steps led downward to what Vincent estimated to be several stories below the earth.

As the group hesitantly followed the resolute Christopher, they were able to spread out and by the time their host had reached the base level of the cavern several remained aloof and mesmerized only partly into the descent.

"How was this place . . . formed?" William gasped, uncertain if he were looking at a manmade marvel or natural occurrence.

Christopher spoke while walking toward a large wooden crate sitting upon the cool ground on the opposite end of the cavern. "The space itself was carved by the Romans over a thousand years ago. They recognized that this place had a certain aura and tried their best to understand it."

"And the Priory was built afterward," William concluded.

Christopher nodded. "Generations have lived and worked here endeavoring to learn as much as possible about the power of this place. I feel that we are becoming closer to that knowledge with your presence."

With the entire group now gathered, the true impressiveness of the space could be realized. Dim light shone and reflected from the planes of chiseled stone surrounding them, broken by roots and softer textures. The ceiling of the cavern, which certainly lay far beneath the Priory's foundations, looked to be of sufficient height to hide the entire citadel from their perspective.

"This is where the relics are kept," Robert concluded, noticing that there was a series of wooden doors encircling the perimeter of the expanse. The chest that Christopher approached was one of only a few utilitarian objects break the plane of the otherwise magnificently uniform hard-packed floor.

"Yes, and prime among them is this," their host punctuated by lifting the massive lid and setting a rod to prop it open.

Vincent and those near enough to him peered in. Christopher produced a scroll of fabric, fully the width of the chest itself, devoid of any ornamental or superfluous trappings. It appeared completely plain until he and Robert suspended it from its unfurled corners, allowing it to flatten into a truly magnificent display.

Beautifully depicted in the center of the tapestry was a building unmistakable as the Priory of Vale. Scattered in what initially seemed to be haphazard fashion were four other unfamiliar locales. The group looked on in awe.

"If you stand back and look at the entire tapestry, it has the shape of a diamond," James volunteered from the middle of the group.

The perceptive archer knight had produced a point of major importance, as even Christopher stood back a few paces to see for himself.

To the right of the Priory was a magnificent stone tower, built among dense trees and vegetation in a manner to suggest that it had not so much been constructed but had emerged from the earth as a supernatural appendage of some sort. Across the fabric to the left was a cave set in an arid surrounding noteworthy because a large natural spring lay to one side and three trees in a triangular formation formed a boundary around it. Then, on the upper edge, a graveyard on a hill broke the otherwise pleasant scenery. There were several individual stones depicted, but any detail that may have been incorporated into the design had long since deteriorated. These scenes captured the attention and curiosity of the men gathered but it was the final image toward the bottom fringes of the tapestry that most were drawn to.

While the four scenes above certainly were meant to evoke a specific location, the final depiction toward the bottom was a symbolic rendering of a crusader's cross not unlike those adorning the tunics of many in attendance. There was an object entwined about the cross of some indefinite design. Several took ventures as to its shape which resembled at best a twisted vine or thick sprig of vegetation with thorns and protuberances along its surface. Vincent was silent as his allies spoke, and stepped back, sliding a hand close to his chest. He knew without needing to look that the form wrapped around the cruciform image was that of the silver dragon about his neck.

XI

"It is thought that the tapestry represents a map of sorts," Christopher explained. "Perhaps this is why Lord Gallock seeks it."

"A map of what?" William inquired.

"This place has an unidentifiable power," Robert mused, referencing their host's exposition. "It is possible that this tapestry connects locations that have similar characteristics."

"It is sufficient to say that we must keep him from gaining possession of the tapestry until we understand more fully what is its significance," Vincent contributed, rejoining the gathered men.

"But we have no way to stop him if he brings the strength of his numbers to bear on us," William answered.

"Perhaps we should flee with the tapestry," Martin suggested.

The group pondered this idea.

"We will at some point need to confront Lord Gallock," Vincent countered.

"We may be able to fall back to Ballecetine to make our stand," Martin amended.

"Surely Lord Gallock does not know of these caverns?" Robert plied.

This introduced a novel idea in the captain's mind. Why would Gallock hesitate with far superior forces if he knew the tapestry to be contained within? Why not move with all his might to destroy the opposition and take what he wanted?

"He may not, but there is one thing that we can count on," Vincent surmised. "We know that he is afraid of sending his forces in to retrieve the tapestry, or he certainly would have laid waste to the Priory by this time. He has superior numbers to easily take it."

"Then why are we still here?" Robert asked.

Vincent held up the Damascus Sword.

"He sent the eagles to know for certain if the bearer of the Damascus Sword was within," Christopher connected. "This is why he hesitates now. He fears the Damascus Sword."

"Yes," Vincent answered. "And we should use that to our advantage until he formulates another plan to advance."

The remainder of the evening was spent in shifts. Two men stood watch while the rest slept. When it was Vincent's turn to rest for a few hours, he fell into a fitful slumber punctuated by his restless mind.

During one such episode, while he was floating between consciousness and sleep, a cloudlike sensation enveloped his senses and Vincent shook himself awake in a strange setting. He felt a familiarity with his previous visions, though unlike those experiences a strong sense of permeating color overwhelmed him.

His environment was indistinct, and even details such as his corporeal presence and extremities lacked definition but everything before him was bathed in a soothing and penetrating emerald green. Amid his sensory overload, a voice whispered through the expanse.

. . . he is aware . . .

Vincent's ears detected the sounds but, like the rest of his body, lacked the faculties to hold focus long enough to understand what was being said.

. . . not long now . . .

He could differentiate this second expression from the first enough to know two separate individuals were speaking. They were female.

. . . can I touch him . . .

A cloudy apparition coalesced before him, vaguely human in outline. It had what appeared to be appendages resembling arms and legs but the closer it came the more Vincent felt his senses numb. He was only aware of its continued presence by a slightly brighter patch of color passing before his eyes and then he jumped awake, startling the men at his side who also rested on the upper level of the citadel.

It was almost dawn.

Christopher strode into view, having just emerged from the lower levels of the keep, and Vincent moved to intercept him at once.

"The tapestry is secured," Christopher announced.

Several allies were now present and the few who were attending to duties below steadily filed through the door. Soon all remaining ten men gathered around the Damascus Sword.

"We cannot remain here if we value our safety," Vincent began. "Lord Gallock is in possession of a power that is exerting influence over this place, possibly over his men. Until we stop him, we will be forever fighting this effect until none of us remain."

The group listened intently, Martin knowing more than the rest what strategy had formed in his captain's mind.

"We will form two parties of five and attempt to gain access into Redmont's camp and eliminate the source before the invasion force has a chance to act," Vincent concluded. "Each party is to arm themselves with sufficient arrows to strike from a distance if the opportunity presents itself."

At this, Christopher and Martin gathered up the longbows and an ample supply of arrows for the men. Vincent divided them into two groups; one led by himself with Robert, Christopher and two of Christopher's men, and the other comprised of Martin, James, William and the last two remaining allies of their host.

"Your group should circle the flank of the camp, much as you began earlier," Vincent directed Martin, William and James' group. "We will approach from the other side."

The two commanders embraced elbows wordlessly without much fanfare, having proven mettle sufficiently to make further conversation irrelevant.

The morning sun rose as Martin led his group warily more and more distant from the Priory's security. Each carried a longbow with arrow at the ready for a preemptive strike, which could account for an initial volley of six missiles with James' armament taken into consideration. They stepped carefully, still in sight of the other group until it crested a small hill and disappeared.

Smoke rose lazily from the enemy camp, in no state of fear from the unknown advance of less than a dozen men. As more details of the setting became visible, James motioned toward the horizon to their right and directed Martin's attention yonder.

"What is that?" Martin winced toward the brightening landscape.

"It appears to be two individuals," James replied, having demonstrated superior visual acuity among the group previously.

The five stalled, still certain of their stealth in regards to Redmont, and observed as two figures on foot struck out on a path vaguely toward them but certainly away from the enemy camp. Martin began moving slowly toward them when motion upon the periphery caused a sudden halt. Three mounted riders had left the camp and were moving to intercept the two individuals, who were now fleeing upon the main road which led directly to the Priory. Martin, as well as the others in his group, concluded that persons valuable enough to be pursued by their opponent were by default also worthy of their intervention.

The five men broke into a run, inwardly calculating the moment of no return, upon which they would be visible to the enemy and would have only a short margin to carry out their ambush without risking a messenger returning to the enemy camp and alerting the entire group of their presence. As they ran, the two persons of interest became more distinct. One was an adult, toting a small child in tow, nearly carrying her airborne from the urgency of the flight. Martin was first to stop, take aim, and fire over the heads of the approaching refugees. His arrow struck true and fell the lead mounted pursuer.

This was the decisive moment. Would one or both of the remaining Redmont aggressors turn and regroup with a larger force? Before a decision could be reached, three more arrows and one bolt flew on tracks destined for valor and in short order the plain lay littered with three corpses. Martin and his group stood stationary, always casting their attention toward the origin and expecting more emissaries to arrive at any moment.

As they pondered the next move, the rescued individuals approached heaving and panting in fear and relief. The adult of the pair removed her dark green hood to a flaming mane of thick red hair cascading downward and over her torso and green tunic.

"My name is Denise," she introduced herself after catching her breath. Martin detected a decidedly Gaelic accent to her speech.

As she spoke, the diminutive half of the duo also removed her hood. "Thank you for rescuing us," the small girl squeaked.

Martin bent low to one knee to observe something unique about this young girl, who could not have been much older than six or seven years. She had mousy and unkempt brown hair but parting their strands with a piercing and adamant defiance were eyes the color of the brightest emerald he had ever seen.

"My name is Stephanie," she offered, meeting his gaze.

In Martin's odd silence, James spoke up.

"We should seek cover at once," he suggested.

The group made quick time to a nearby grove from whence they could converse in security but also have one eye toward the enemy camp.

"We are inhabitants from Westford, just over those hills," Denise explained, flattening the pleats in her dark green dress. Stephanie, always at her side, was eyeing up their rescuers with a calculating air that made Martin a bit uneasy.

"Lord Gallock has made it his base of operations," she continued. This pulled Martin's attention finally from the girl to the conversation at hand.

"I knew there had to be a headquarters nearby," he echoed.

"What is the state of matters there?" William asked.

Denise nodded ruefully. "The soldiers have pillaged and destroyed everything that cannot be eaten or pressed into service. Many of the men were forced into labor."

"We escaped just as things got worse," Stephanie continued.

Martin mulled this information. Now, they had a duality of purpose but rather than conflicting, he hoped that solving one dilemma would also conclude the other.

"If we can eliminate Lord Gallock's hold over this place, perhaps the liberation of Westford will follow," William verbalized the very notion in Martin's mind.

"Yes," Martin agreed, casting his glance toward the enemy camp. "Many things will be made clear once that situation is resolved."

Vincent stood at the zenith of one of the small hills overlooking Redmont's camp. There were assorted groups of men-at-arms and mounted riders patrolling the main access points into the camp as expected. Routinely, a captain would circumnavigate the various posts and demand a report from the attending sentry. To hide its effect from view, the Damascus Sword had been wrapped in a thick cloth and strapped to Vincent's back. This would not be a major inconvenience, he thought, as the longbow in his grasp would needs be exhausted of its ammunition before hand-to-hand combat would become the emphasis of any skirmish.

"Perhaps there," Christopher suggested, pointing toward a corner of the camp partially hidden by trees.

"No doubt there are patrols that sweep the woods, but we could get close enough to assemble some sort of attack," Robert concurred.

"That seems to be the best option available to us at the moment," Vincent agreed.

The five paced carefully on the hidden slopes of the rolling hills. Periodically taking a detour to assess the state of the enemy camp, Vincent halted at a point roughly halfway to their destination.

"What is it?" Robert inquired, joining him upon a nearby knoll.

Ahead, a detachment of three mounted riders left the confines of the camp in haste and disappeared behind the landscape. They were traveling in the same direction that Vincent knew the other party to be headed.

"Have they spotted the others?" Christopher intoned, also joining them.

"Possibly," Vincent mused, but then turned his attention back toward the camp. There were trios of mounted riders assembling all about the periphery of the group.

"They are foraging," Christopher concluded, watching the same developments unfold.

"There are not many resources in the immediate surroundings. They must be pulling supplies from nearby towns," Vincent clarified.

Then a larger group of riders broke the plane on the opposite end of the camp. They were towing carts full of food, weapons and imprisoned captives.

"What villages are nearby?" Robert asked.

"Westford is just over those hills," Christopher answered, pointing toward the origin of the returning marauders. "It is substantial enough to supply a small force for some time and it has ample water supplies."

"We must continue toward the main camp and avoid the groups of patrols," Vincent concluded. "If we can eliminate Lord Gallock's hold over this place, some answers will be found in Westford."

The five walked cautiously, still able to hide sufficiently but taking a wider arc toward the concealing trees. They would have to cross one of the main thoroughfares through the countryside at some point to reach their goal, and that was what concerned Vincent the most. The trios of riders began departing at a speed that suggested an urgent objective at hand, however; and the group gambled that they were not mere roving patrols sent to scour the surrounding environment.

When the trees were roughly a bowshot away, Vincent halted the party and raised his longbow, arrow in place. By happenstance, one of the groups of riders had stopped between them and the small woods, close enough that they were able to allow their horses to drink from a small pond at the edge of the forest.

Wordlessly, the group trained upon the unsuspecting riders and prepared to fire as one. Just as Vincent was about to release, motion behind the targets caused him to hesitate. Several mounted individuals were occupying the very woods from which Vincent had hoped to plan an offensive. He slowly lowered his bow as the rest did likewise and watched as the initial group of three moved on and away from them, all the while unknowing the fate they had evaded.

"If we attack now, we will alert all the riders in this area," Vincent explained. "Patience will be the better part of valor until these men ride off."

The next few moments agonized and drew onward for what seemed like hours. Finally, two additional groups of three left the disputed woods and rode out of sight. As they waited, a new strategy formed in the captain's mind. With so many agents of Redmont absent in the countryside, perhaps this was the time to strike at the heart. He noticed that a faint glow had emanated from the enveloped blade strapped to his back as they approached, so Lord Gallock himself was surely still within the confines of the now sparsely populated camp.

"With so many gone, now is the time to infiltrate the camp," Vincent shared with the party. "Have a ready supply of arrows, and be prepared to use your blade in close quarters," he bolstered.

With this, the five struck out on a path directly into the heart of the enemy. A few straggling patrols took note of them but were silenced before sounding an alarm. Vincent and Christopher reloaded their bows. They were but steps from the perimeter of the outer tents and smoldering fires when Robert alerted them to the increasing light cast from the Damascus Sword. They were getting close now.

Three more sentries fell without a sound as the central field tent came into view. At this point, the party encountered its first resistance and a larger group of seven men advanced from just beyond the far side of the main tent. They looked to have hastily armed themselves and even so two of their number were able to fire crossbows before Vincent's group was able to return fire. One bolt skimmed Vincent's right shoulder and careened to the side while the sickening impact of metal into flesh registered in his senses from behind. The melee was about to engulf them and the enemy party drew swords as there was no longer room nor time to draw and fire in return.

Vincent threw down the bow and loosened the strap around his shoulder, about to brandish the blinding blade when three streaks of wood sliced through the opponent's ranks, each blindsiding and felling one. This caused enough confusion to allow Vincent's party to return fire and completely dispatch the remainder of their number. Martin, William and James ran onto the scene as Vincent's party counted the loss of one of Christopher's men in the ambush.

"Captain," William spoke, pointing.

The Damascus Sword was at full brilliance, brighter than any had seen yet. Vincent deduced that this was the purpose for William's warning but quickly learned that he was indicating beyond his position, toward the main field tent.

In its entrance stood two heavily armored knights flanking Lord Gallock himself.

XII

Vincent raised the Damascus Sword as he turned to face the focus of their nearly successful campaign.

"You possess that which is mine," Lord Gallock stated in purely factual cadence that ignored his being outnumbered better than two-to-one.

Vincent moved to strike before the opposition could muster an offensive, but just as he shifted his stance to advance, strong arms gripped his forearms and held him fast. It was Christopher, Robert, and his men themselves restraining him. Before the audacity of the action could impress itself upon him, Vincent cast a gaze toward the only ally that had not betrayed. Martin stood aghast and distant but swiftly calculated that some unseen force had taken hold of all save him. Lord Gallock advanced, unknowing that one had escaped his power, just as Martin wrenched the crossbow from his paralyzed ally and loosed its last projectile. It was off-balance and ill-aimed, but the bolt struck the astonished aggressor's left forearm, which shook his hold on the knights momentarily enough for Vincent to wrestle free and bring the unearthly blade down upon the neck of the staggering enemy. Body and head fell separately as the entranced men about him awoke as from a long slumber.

"What has happened?" William gasped.

The rest of the group shook themselves, looking about in confusion. The pair of armored Redmont knights before them did likewise, affirming Martin's assumption that Gallock had exercised some form of control over those around him to accomplish his goal.

"Sir . . . I . . ." Robert reeled, looking to his hands.

"You were not in control of yourselves," Vincent assured the dumbfounded group. "Lord Gallock has had a hold on all those around him."

The Redmont knights removed their helmets, speechless. As the newly-awakened knights loyal to Vincent had just experienced, the time in which Lord Gallock had controlled them created a blank space in their memories. They were no more aware of their actions while under his influence than if they had been unconscious, which was disconcerting for the small amount of time they had felt the effect but was certain to be debilitating for those under his command for a longer span.

"You should gather your men and return to Redmont," Vincent directed the confused guards. "I fear that Lord Gallock's effect may have created a great sense of confusion and uncertainty in your land."

The attending knights wandered off, as pockets of similarly sluggish men loyal to the late lord joined them and small groups began forming about the lost camp. As they did so, Vincent and Martin held a meeting near the deceased enemy's corpse.

"You felt none of the same effect as the others?" Vincent inquired.

"None," Martin answered in disbelief.

The group stood in silence, Vincent absently noticing how the Damascus Sword had lost its shine after the death of Lord Gallock.

"The sword," James interjected.

All eyes turned to him.

"When we were on the ship, you touched the sword," James answered, walking up to the pair.

Vincent held the blade up to his scrutiny.

"Interesting," Robert mumbled. "Lord Gallock could not control the one wielding the blade nor one who had touched it."

Christopher had joined the small gathering, deep in thought. "I believe it is time for myself and . . . what allies of mine remain . . . to look into this matter further."

Robert turned to face the priory host.

"I believe we will learn more if we enter the nearby town of Westford," Martin supplied, noting Christopher's confusion over the absence of two of their party. "While we were investigating, we rescued two refugees from the village. Perhaps we could return them and learn the state of Ballecetine there. Currently they are hiding with two of the men from the Priory in the woods."

"Robert, will you accompany Christopher and his men to the Priory? Find what answers you can from the tapestry and delve into the mystery of this effect with all the elements at your disposal," Vincent issued. "Meanwhile, the rest of us will return the refugees and learn what we can in Westford."

This was agreeable to all, and just as the groups split, Martin looked down, noticing that the body of Lord Gallock had disappeared. Christopher and Robert crouched to the ground where his body had been. Not a drop of blood nor impression remained to attest to the existence of the fallen lord. Vincent assessed the situation from above, noting also that the blood had dissipated from the blade used to slay Lord Gallock. Not a blemish nor nick marred the pristine surface of the silver sword as it glinted in the rising light of day.

A brief sweep through the enemy camp confirmed that it was deserted. Vincent led the bulk of the group through abandoned dwellings. Discarded weapons and various implements littered the ground as though the camp had been inhabited by ghosts. Not a living soul other than his men traversed the wasteland until they reached the outer perimeter. Vincent and Martin walked side by side at the vanguard, but it was James who saw it first from behind them.

"It is the old man from the galley," Vincent announced.

He was astride a horse, certainly not of his possession, waiting upon the course ahead and between their current location and the refugees' woods.

Vincent stole a glance at the Damascus Sword. As before, it began to emit a faint light at first and then a growing luminosity as they approached. He kept the blade in hand as they reached speaking distance.

"You have done well, my son," the interloper called out.

Vincent thought that his appearance had improved considerably since their last meeting when his health seemed in a state of concern. Now, his posture was more stately and breath came easily in contrast to the coughing fits and spasms that had punctuated his speech last time.

"What is your connection to this blade?" Vincent demanded as his proximity and ire grew.

"I shall be watching you, my son," the man replied as he turned the reins in his hand as to depart.

Vincent and the others moved to intercept him but only too late realized the folly of their actions, as the enigmatic figure disappeared characteristically before their faces with the beginnings of a malicious smile forming across his countenance. Also, as expected, the Damascus Sword lost its glow instantly as the man slipped from their sight.

"This is becoming tiresome," Vincent expressed, sheathing the lengthy weapon as the group completed its journey to the woods.

The stationed priory guards emerged as the party drew near. A few minutes' exposition regarding the splitting of their forces and duties to be performed at the Priory called them back into action and they departed in haste to join the dwindling remainder of their number.

As they left, Martin peered into the woods and spied the refugees sitting near a stream that flowed into the very reservoir that the mounted Redmont knights had visited only moments ago. Denise stood, sensing the presence of those approaching, while the girl remained close to the water's surface.

"Lord Gallock's hold over the land has been removed," Vincent declared, avoiding the unnatural circumstances of the encounter. "We would be very interested in any news you have of the state of the region, as we are just returning from abroad."

"I am Denise," the adult refugee introduced, bowing slightly. "My companion . . ." she trailed, turning toward the creek and unsuccessfully beckoning the girl's attention.

The stalled pleasantries allowed a moment's pause during which Vincent felt a strange stirring within. Denise was about to retrieve the preoccupied girl, but Vincent took the initiative.

He crouched to her perspective and peered into the clear water. After a few moments, Stephanie turned to him but Vincent sensed an indescribable aura about the young girl. She gazed at and through his eyes with the most penetrating light that he had ever experienced. The captain marveled at the clarity of her perceptive green eyes with almost as much confusion as her first utterance in his presence created.

"Unus es tu?"

The first task to be accomplished at the nearly abandoned Priory was the last respect for the dead. Christopher and Robert labored with the help of the last attendants to give some semblance of a proper burial to those slain in the clashes with the eagles and Redmont soldiers.

"I did not know these men long," Christopher memorialized, "but what I do know of them was their tenacity to maintain the memories of the past and their connection to the present."

It was fitting, Robert thought, that the current predicament had cost them so dearly if the sought artifacts beneath them were indeed as precious as they seemed. This bolstered and strengthened him as they completed the manual labor of remembering the dead and transitioned to the important work of contemplating the meaning of all that had happened for the future.

Five men retired to the main hall to rest and regain their strength for the upcoming task. They partook in a small meal silently, each recounting the surreal and supernatural events that had recently transpired.

"There is a tome of some weight that might aid us in the search for meaning in these things," Christopher declared, breaking the uneasy silence.

"I as well have collected a great deal of writings from the East and the principalities of the Crusader armies of the last centuries," Robert added. "If we are fortunate, there may be an intersection where our sources align and we can deduce something of these strange powers that have emerged in our land."

With this, the five men hastened to the underground caverns to pore over decades and centuries of collected paraphernalia on every topic related to the Paladin and the Damascus Sword.

Vincent tensed as the young girl paused then blinked and introduced herself as though she had not just spoken Latin as clear as the brook at their feet.

"My name is Stephanie," she squeaked, then stood, turned and rejoined Denise.

Vincent rose slowly, uncertain of what he had just witnessed. He rejoined the small group as Denise expounded on her limited knowledge of events in Ballecetine.

"What I know is that one week ago, Lord Gallock and his men commandeered our village and pressed us into service for the support of his army," she began, patting Stephanie on the head. "Stephanie and I managed to escape but were never able to find anyone to help us."

"Perhaps the freed inhabitants of Westford could inform us as to the state of matters in Ballecetine," Martin suggested vaguely toward an inattentive and preoccupied Vincent.

James and William also detected their captain's lost state.

"Yes, we should make haste for Westford," Vincent concluded, rejoining the conversation. "We will reunite you with your family and lend what aid we can."

"Oh, I am the only family Stephanie has," Denise countered. "And at that only a guardian for the girl. She came to me one stormy evening six years ago, abandoned by a stranger who was passing through our village."

As she spoke, the girl cleft to the lengths of Denise's dress. Martin cast Vincent a glance, knowing that he also had sensed something unique about the girl.

The group left the safety of the small woods and began the trek toward Westford. On foot it would take a fair portion of the day, so there was ample opportunity for reflection and conversation in the relative calm that followed the tense confrontations from earlier.

"I cannot help but feel that our meeting these refugees is not by chance," Martin divulged as he and Vincent had taken the lead of the procession by a wide enough margin not to be heard by the rest.

Vincent nodded in agreement. "I have learned to assume that nothing is happening by chance since leaving the Holy Land."

"There is a maturity to the small girl's manners that betrays her appearance," Martin added.

"That is for certain," Vincent concurred. "When I stooped low to greet her, she spoke to me in Latin."

This did garner Martin's attention.

"*Unus es tu?*" Vincent recounted.

Martin translated in his mind momentarily while Vincent did so verbally.

"Are you the one?"

XIII

Aside from periodic breaks during the warmest part of the early afternoon, the party made excellent time and soon the hamlet of Westford appeared upon the horizon, nestled in a natural valley fed by streams. The village's geography made it a perfect target for a traveling army.

William and James conversed often with the newcomers, while Vincent and Martin used the time to observe the girl and come to some understanding as to her odd behavior. For all their scrutiny, Stephanie acted, talked and behaved completely as expected for a young girl and exhibited no more of the duality of persona that Vincent had witnessed earlier. Martin could not define his exact concerns only that her piercing stare seemed to him unnatural. The young girl jumped, skipped and even attempted to incorporate the stoic knights in her frolics, deepening their fascination with her personality.

"We live here, in the outskirts of the village," Denise announced as they approached a bustling thoroughfare into the diminutive town.

There was no sign of Redmont in the vicinity, but several of the harried townsfolk took notice of the party and came to welcome their lost pair and learn the identities of the armed escort. Upon learning that Vincent and Martin were returning knights, a group hastened to the square.

"Lord Gallock was able to control us by some supernatural force," explained a spokesman for the gathered people. "He made us supply his men and aid in the planning of a raid on the Priory of Vale."

"So you were conscious of your actions during this effect?" Martin queried as one unknowing of its power.

"We were," answered another. "We didn't know what we were doing. It was as if we were acting by our own will."

This did seem to conflict with what Vincent had witnessed in his men earlier. Perhaps extending control over such a large group weakened its hold somehow, he reasoned. Then, a novel idea entered his mind.

"Do you recall any conversation or discussion about the state of matters in Ballecetine while you were under his influence?"

"Yes, many of the men among Redmont's ranks were captured from Ballecetine," answered the spokesman again. At this point, a familiar face entered their circle and spoke.

"Sir, I encountered this effect as soon as we came onto our home soil," announced Sir Stipe, the envoy Vincent had sent ahead to Ballecetine upon disembarking from the ship at Iden.

A rushed reunion of embraces followed, as a small group of about a dozen men emerged from the growing crowd, all from the Ballecetine group. It seemed to Vincent that the mood was rather subdued rather than joyous.

"What news have you?" he prodded.

"While we were under the control of Lord Gallock," Stipe prefaced, meeting the downward glances of the other allied men in the group, "we were charged with carrying Lord West and his daughter to the gulag *Mora Fenris* at the edge of our land."

The news struck them as though physically, but Vincent continued the examination.

"So what is the state of Ballecetine itself?"

"Gallock left it unharmed," Stipe revealed.

Vincent suspected that Gallock's offensive was intended to coerce Vincent to relinquish the Damascus Sword by using the leverage of hostages. The fact that his home had escaped destruction by the mysterious power Gallock had held confirmed his suspicion that all things centered around the sword in his grasp.

"With the elimination of Lord Gallock and his control, we should seek to set events right in the land," Martin suggested.

"The four of us will ride to *Mora Fenris* to return Lord West and Diana to their proper places," Vincent stated. "Sir Stipe, aid these townspeople but do not hesitate to return to Ballecetine as soon as possible to assess what matters need attention there."

By this point, it was early evening, and the three men in Vincent's party knew enough to surmise that the captain did not intend to wait until first light to set out.

Denise and Stephanie returned to a warm homecoming. Their abode had been preserved, and the girl leaped onto her bed mat. Well-wishers and concerned elders made the rounds in a joyous promenade that their village had been spared and saved by the returning crusaders. As the sun sank lower and lower in the sky, a lone horse-mounted figure rode past, halting momentarily near the entrance.

Vincent shifted as to dismount, but then thought better and slid back into his saddle. There was something about the girl Stephanie that beckoned him almost as strongly as the pull to see Diana again. He heard the young girl's voice from within the dwelling and contented himself with the reassurance that when all was concluded he would come back to visit Westford again. One thing he knew; this was not to be their last meeting.

Vincent and Martin knew the devotion of time that was being expected of their non-Ballecetine counterparts. A brief conversation was all that was required for William and James to reassert their duty to the overall cause, knowing full well that the end of Lord Gallock did not mean the end to the strange mystery and power of the Damascus Sword. No, the duo were adamant that their homes and families would wait until the completion of their mission and greater purpose as members of the *Damascene Order*.

It was dusk when the party first halted its pace. Vincent directed the group to rest for a short time, and they would retake the trail during the night to arrive at first light. Any obstacles or hindrances to their ultimate goal of the return of the Lord and daughter to the realm would be met with the early rays of the sun at their backs.

Minutes turned to hours. Hours passed as minutes. Robert, Christopher and the remaining attendants of the Priory labored in the caverns tirelessly unaware of the passage of time. The most recent evidence had been found by the newcomer, attesting to the novelty of new eyes on old documents.

"I have found a brief history of a man named Anakhron," he revealed. "He seems to have been a figure of some importance in this area."

Christopher left his work and joined Robert.

"It is in Latin," Robert commented, less as a detriment to the endeavor and more as an encouragement.

Christopher leaned inward, scrutinizing the document.

"Over a thousand years ago, Anakhron was a Roman centurion who was charged with finding . . ." he trailed off.

"It becomes difficult to read," Robert commented as Christopher attempted to mentally fill gaps and extrapolate from the incomplete parchment.

"The Romans were mining in this area, and the very cavern we inhabit now is their work," Christopher reiterated.

"Could they have been looking for riches here?" Robert inquired. "This land was *Provincia Britannia* for a time."

Christopher seemed to be in some doubt as to the purely economical bent of such an expedition. "There had to be something of value here, something that transcended monetary pursuits."

Robert set the document down and, turning, held up another that seemed to be a companion in both age and condition to the first.

"Here, in this provincial map, is an inscription that I cannot decipher," Robert spoke, producing a crude representation that was clearly the channel between England and the Continent.

"Interesting," Christopher mused, holding the new example up to the flickering firelight. "Do you see how this edge is rough," he ran fingers up and down the left margin of the uneven paper. "There must be a companion that completes it."

Robert saw also that the edge Christopher had indicated was not worn as the others were, indicating the edge of the parchment; it was torn carelessly and more recently than its manufacture.

All hands were set to the work of finding the matching edge to the map. Both Christopher and Robert felt that they had stumbled upon something significant.

The floor of the caverns began to resemble a patchwork in short order. What had been discovered as potentially a single scrap that had met with an unfortunate severance culminated in a massive quilt of varying shapes, sizes and textures. Doubtlessly several hours were spent in frenzied and silent diligence and when it was completed, Christopher stood back to gain perspective on its scope.

"The stairs!" Robert called.

Instantly, the five laborers rushed to the stairs toward the surface, from whence they attained a birds-eye view of their work. With scattered writing adorning much of its perimeter and interior, and a myriad of creases, folds and tears notwithstanding, the assembled puzzle was uncannily familiar.

"It is a map of the coastline of England," Christopher noted, "and bears the same proportions and locations as the tapestry."

"And this," Robert indicated, pointing downward, "what is this?"

Christopher and Robert descended to what would correspond to the western edge of the assembled papers, careful always not to cause too much stir to jumble them again.

"Perhaps comparing it directly to the tapestry would benefit our study," Christopher stated, retrieving the precious artifact from its chest. When he had unfurled it and set it beside the patchwork, their similarities were undeniable.

"It is as though someone created the tapestry to record the information on these sheets," Robert marveled.

"In abbreviated form," Christopher noted. "See how the parchments contain writing where the tapestry is only the visual representations and main visuals."

Robert scrutinized the left edge of the tapestry, where the cave surrounded by three trees was depicted. Corresponding to this location on the larger, more detailed map was a similar picture. Written in script near the base of the trees was an odd message. Christopher read it aloud:

Where wolves delay

"What does this mean?" Christopher wondered. For some reason this, separate from all other imagery and mystery placed before them, attracted the attention of the group.

"Wolves . . . wolves . . ." Robert trailed, leaving in a bit of haste turbulent to the scattered map.

Christopher straightened them silently, still deep in thought, as Robert returned with a scroll from among his possessions.

"The Wolves' Delay," Robert connected, unrolling a volume the length of his forearm. It was beautifully illuminated with powerful imagery of the predatory canines taking respite from a hunt around the edges of a natural spring. The scale of the depictions was such that the illustrator had spent his time and effort on the animals, but the outline of the three trees from the tapestry and map were telling even though the cave itself was not present. The only words to adorn the otherwise brilliant document were the words Robert continually repeated, alongside another penned expression. Robert read them aloud:

The Wolves' Delay
Mora Fenris

Four horses broke the horizon. Vincent and Martin were first to see the outer buildings and wall, but it was James who called their attention upward. Carrion birds circled high over the position of the prison and Vincent held a momentary pang of trepidation until his eyes were able to focus and ascertain that these were normal creatures and not the supernatural birds of prey that they had before encountered.

They redoubled their pace in anticipation, taking no note that the Damascus Sword tied upon the captain's back had begun again to shine with greater brilliance the closer they came to their destination.

"*Mora Fenris* is the location of an old dungeon near the edge of Ballecetine," Christopher offered. "Perhaps the trees and cave existed there before the building of the prison."

"Or the prison encompasses the cave itself," Robert countered.

"I have not been there, but from what I understand it is built primarily below ground, so that is a possibility," Christopher added.

The astute historians stood in a moment of silent contemplation. It was a foregone conclusion that at some point they would need to travel to this location to learn the reason for its inclusion on the highly-sought tapestry.

Being a native of Ballecetine, Vincent was aware of the prison's existence, but its far-flung nature eliminated it from use by his principality.   He could not recount a situation where he or anybody that he knew had visited it, and it was this state of disuse that concerned him; there was no telling what awaited them within.

Vultures circled and cackled overhead as Vincent and the group stopped at the main gate of the outer wall. Dismounting, the captain found the barrier falling off its posts and cast them aside. Martin, James and William descended from their steeds and the four walked warily into the open courtyard.

It was at this point that Vincent drew the blade and noticed its light, though not blinding as when in Lord Gallock's presence, was growing by the pace as they approached the inner structure. There was no doubt now; both the fate of his Lord and love would be ascertained in this barren place.

When the party had traversed roughly half the distance to the main building, Vincent witnessed a strange occurrence. The blade's intensity had continued to grow as the four walked, but as they drew closer and closer to their goal, it began to fade. By the time they stood at the entrance, which was in a similar state of disrepair as the gates, the Damascus Sword had reverted to its normal state, striking and entrancing as it was.

The entrance to the prison was nothing more than a worn-down shack of a building that led downward. The door was deteriorated and held no locking mechanism. Even if it had, Vincent could easily have pried it from its frame. A brief survey of the surroundings confirmed that there had been no activity here in some time. Stables were overgrown and ill-maintained, large portions of the outer wall had crumbled, and even the trees in this desolate place looked the worse for wear.

Trees.

Vincent's attention flew to a trio of sickly trunks not ten paces behind the entrance to the lower levels. Instantly, his mind connected the imagery from the tapestry. He led the party to the small stand of vegetation and noted that the natural spring that had accompanied the illustration had likely dried up, but where the cave had been located could only correspond to the entrance.

"*Mora Fenris* is the cave from the tapestry," Vincent blurted.

The rest of the group realized the similarities, William circling the trees while James kept his eyes always upward and outward, for the vultures maintained their stoic patrol of the skies above them.

"We are meant to travel to each of the locations on the tapestry to discover the meaning of the Damascus Sword," Vincent continued.

Inwardly, the captain wondered if they should dare enter the prison. It might prove more advantageous to reconnect with the group at the Priory and formulate a strategy in full force, he reasoned. Then, the entire party could put their combined knowledge and might toward a resolution.

This contemplation was put aside rather quickly, however, when Vincent felt an empowering chill rush through the handle of the Damascus Sword. It raised the hair on his arm and instinctively tightened the tendons in his hand around the weapon. Vincent felt the urge to release his grasp, as the cold was becoming unbearable, but he could not. He lost feeling in his fingers and, subsequently his right hand.

"What is it?" Martin inquired, noticing the change in his friend's demeanor.

"The sword . . . I . . . can't . . ." was as much as the captain could utter before the numbing effect engulfed his arm and crept up and down his spine. His final vision before succumbing entirely and losing consciousness was that of his allies rushing to cushion his fall.

XIV

I have him now.
Wait, he is still too weak.
A sensation of floating.
Motion.
Light from an indistinct origin.
Warmth.
He is strong enough for this.
Stop, you are killing him!
Waves of nausea overtook Vincent. He opened his eyes to a mad swirl of color and indescribable chaos. He shut his eyes tightly to regain his composure.
He must know!
Not now.
Vincent felt his lungs screaming, but no sound. His hands tightened into fists, but nothing was within reach. Legs flailed and kicked into an impossible nothingness around him and reality slipped away from his mind. He was floating but not falling, living but not breathing; sensing and yet blind, deaf and silent.
You seek me.
Vincent heard this in his mind, unsure if any of his senses still functioned or if he still possessed a physical body.
I know you.
Attempting to speak was impossible. Vincent prodded his mind to answer.
"Who are you?"

It grows stronger. You must prevail.

"Who are you?"

A pause followed his second and, what he had hoped was more authoritative, questioning thought. This time, Vincent had the abstract impression that the passionless voice relayed regret and pity.

You cannot know.

With a rush and a gasp, Vincent sat up to the immediate surprise of the attending knights. The coldness of the blade had dissipated, and Vincent eyed it closely in a mesmerized state of confusion.

"Sir," James called, as to one distant and oblivious.

"You were completely cold and stiff," William added, wide-eyed.

Martin was about to add his own relief when motion on the periphery caught his attention.

Vincent stood warily and found that his senses and faculties returned immediately as though nothing unusual had occurred.

James pointed toward the wall ahead of them, on the opposite side of the dilapidated courtyard. A mounted figure stood facing them, spear and shield couched as for battle. Vincent took an initial step forward when it occurred to him that there were no means of entry into the courtyard from the direction they were facing; the mounted figure seemed to simply have appeared out of nowhere.

"Behind!" William called.

A similar figure appeared behind them near the wall by the broken gate. As the four stood in bewilderment, two additional mounted soldiers congealed from the air, one in each cardinal direction and all encircling the party of four, though at a distance. They made no advance or offensive motion. It was clear that no one would be allowed to exit the premises.

James stood by, two bolts at the ready should the command be given. William and Martin likewise observed the opposition for any signs of aggression.

"It seems as though we are not meant to leave this place," Vincent surmised, "until we explore below."

Robert had over time learned that the surviving three companions from the Priory were named Galen, Bertrand, and Caine.

As the five of them made preparations to set out for the nearby town of Westford and attempt to rejoin the rest of the party with their newfound discoveries, they paid last respects to the fresh graves of fallen allies. He inwardly felt sorrow that he had not even learned the names of the men who had died, and vowed that his conviction to unravel the mysteries surrounding them would serve as a posthumous honor.

James and William took the lead, entering the descent. Martin and Vincent exchanged concerned looks, each inwardly unwilling to concede the acceptance of the four black knights' unspoken direction. A confrontation was decidedly unwelcome, however, until more could be learned about the significance of this place.

Light emanated from below in the form of several scattered torches lining the walls of the brick and stone-lined staircase. Each man in turn scavenged one of the healthier appearing fixtures and brandished a weapon in his right hand except for Martin who held his torch with his right and sword with his left.

The four descended for nearly three stories, William estimated, and came to a carved stone landing wide enough for all to occupy and not have to stand single-file any longer. The cold surface was the floor of a roughly cube-shaped foyer which offered a thick, wooden door in each of the three directions facing them. Weak light filtered down through the straight and narrow staircase behind them.

"These doors are meant for hard use," William commented, touching each surface in turn.

It was true; whereas all the other furnishings and hardware of the run-down prison had fallen into serious disrepair, these three doors stood in blatant contrast to the passage of time and trial. They were also, William found, securely locked.

"Do we just pick a door?" Martin suggested.

The others, for lack of a better determination, could not disagree.

"Forward," Vincent pronounced.

It took but a few brief moments for William to breach the locking mechanism and push the door inward on heavily resistant hinges. Four torches blazed a clear projection of light into a large open space. Whereas the cavern below the Priory had a ragged and natural atmosphere, the dungeon expanse ahead of them was finished with solid brick and very uniform in appearance. There were many rusted and broken pillars touching either the floor or ceiling randomly throughout, with a few brave structures still complete and spanning the entire height.

"This must be what remains of the holding cells of the prison," James concluded.

No light but the sources in the men's hands filled the space. Each strode warily onto the floor, but it was obvious with a few moment's scrutiny that there was nothing of interest, living or otherwise, to occupy their attention here.

"Two doors remain," Martin offered as the four left the barren room, closing the door behind them.

Next, William unlocked the door to the left of the entrance, if for no other reason than he was in closest proximity to it. This large room was identical to the first, complete with corroding and broken bars strewn about. No one had been held in this prison for some time.

"Something must be hidden here," Vincent lamented as the four again left an empty room, closing the door behind them, and traversed the vestibule quickly toward what was most assuredly the focal point of their search.

William was becoming increasingly accomplished in his lockpicking skills and had the third and final door open in half the time it took him to bypass the first one. Again, disappointingly, a desolate and abandoned cell block greeted their hopeful anticipation. The four stood near the center of the room, breathing in stale air that no living thing had disturbed in some time, in a perplexed mood.

"There *must* be something here," Vincent whispered.

Martin, James and William had dispersed to examining the walls for lack of any other avenue while Vincent remained near the center, attempting to find any defect or irregularity in the floor and ceiling surfaces. For all the wear that time had caused, the basic construction of the prison was sound; chiseled stone and brick still held back the erosion of nature except for a few small roots that had poked through fissures between the joints of some of the blocks.

Then, Vincent remembered when above the Damascus Sword had shone briefly, then dulled, and regained its light as they crossed the courtyard from the wall to the entrance. The rooms they had explored so far reached away from their initial approach. Could it be that whatever force had triggered the Damascus Sword had passed directly under them? If so, there must be more to the prison's layout than what was directly observable.

Vincent wandered toward one of the walls. Just as he was about to reach out and touch the cold stone surface, James called his attention from across the silent expanse.

"What is it?" Vincent answered as all congregated near what they hoped to be an avenue of some discovery.

"It may be nothing, but," James trailed, moving his hand across a row of bricks at shoulder level. Vincent did likewise.

"It feels warmer than the surrounding rock," Vincent mused.

Martin and William explored and concurred.

"The effect extends about four bricks wide," James noted, as the four traced an outline that roughly corresponded to the perimeter of a doorway.

A line, imperceptible unless directly observed, marked the definite boundaries of a portal. William was the first to notice it.

"Here," William traced.

Vincent and Martin leaned the heft of their weight against the stone and, though it did not give way, the faint outline thickened incrementally. They were moving the slab.

"Everyone," Vincent called.

Together, the four men strained and pushed. With backs against the stone, increasing progress was made until the entire width of the brick had recessed within the unknown room on the other side. It took a few more strong pushes, and the cemented barrier slid loose from its frame, teetered momentarily, then fell with a great crash on the other side. It broke into four jagged fragments upon a packed earthen pathway. Vincent and the others stepped out onto its shattered pieces and took in the setting.

The chamber before them was framed entirely with earthen boundaries in great contrast to the manufactured and uniform construction they had just left. No beams or supports traversed the expanses from floor to ceiling, which was roughly equal to that of the finished cells behind them. Instead, massive root systems interlaced and crossed throughout the upper surfaces, obscuring a clear definition of the confines of the space.

The Damascus Sword began to glow faintly at first, and then with increasing light as Vincent entered the hidden room. They were moving away from the base of the descent and toward the point where above the sword had shone briefly.

William and James paced outward, dwindling torches still in hand. The stark background and scenery cast a shadowy uncertainty upon the very ground they trod. Just as James had left arm's reach from the rest, Vincent spotted movement above. Before any could react or call out, one of the roots that supported the ceiling shot downward and laced itself around the archer knight's right forearm. James instinctively fired his crossbow as the thick tendril lifted him upward. William, who was nearest to his side, dropped his sword and grasped James' right foot as it shot upward past him. Both men's torches fell to the floor and darkened instantly, which summoned a uniquely terrifying mood as two bodies thrashed and dangled ever upward in the dying light.

Martin and Vincent rushed to the scene. The Damascus Sword was blazing brightly but through all the clamor, a piercing scream could be heard from some indistinct location above.

"Vincent!"

His pulse quickened.

His senses sharpened.

It was Diana.

XV

Robert and Christopher led the party into the confines of the small village. The group at first stood aloof and distant, observing the meager commerce of their surroundings.

"Hello," a diminutive voice interrupted.

Christopher looked down into the clearest green eyes he had ever seen.

"My name is Stephanie," the young girl offered as though asked.

Robert and the others had begun to wander, looking for informative townsfolk, while Christopher bent to the girl's level, unspeaking.

"What's your name?" Stephanie prodded.

The attendant of Vale remained mesmerized. It took another, separate, introduction to break him from his gaze.

"I see you've met Stephanie," a tall, red-haired woman spoke upon entering the scene.

"Yes . . . I've . . ." Christopher stammered, rising but not taking his eyes from the girl's.

"You must be with the others who came through earlier," Denise continued.

"Yes," Christopher answered, tearing himself back to the present situation. "A group from Ballecetine."

Robert and the others had returned by now, detecting that Christopher had stumbled upon some information.

"Their captain sent the remainder of the men back to Ballecetine," Denise explained. "But he and a few of his men went onward, to *Mora Fenris*."

Upon hearing the focus of their research, the group took special notice.

"*Mora Fenris?*" Christopher nearly shouted. "Why did they decide to go there?"

"While under the control of Lord Gallock, the Lord and daughter of Ballecetine were taken there," Denise responded.

Christopher and the others paused, saying nothing, for several awkward moments.

"Are you going there too?" Stephanie interjected.

Robert cast a concerned look toward Christopher, but he had fallen again into the purest stare of emerald.

The Damascus Sword rose as everyone's attention focused upward. James was dangling precariously, his right hand just touching the slithering surface above him, when the brightness of the blinding blade repelled its interest. Vincent noted that the closer he held the sword toward the roots and vines, the more they shrunk from his advance.

"Where are you?" Vincent shouted into the mass.

No answer was forthcoming, but the vines did release their grip on his men. James hastily reloaded his crossbow, training it upward the instant he was prepared. Martin and William scanned the visible portions of the panoply, hearing and seeing nothing more than their harried captain, who was waving the blade in wide arcs to scatter the obscuring growth. Each time he illuminated a swath of the vegetation, a new pathway to within was revealed, but no terminating surface or explanation as to its origin became clear.

Then, Vincent made a realization. If he were to gain access to the inner windings of the twisting roots, it would be without the Damascus Sword, as the tangled mass retreated and cowered in its proximity. Hastily, he cast the blade to the stone surface and distanced himself from it. Predictably, a probing arm reached down slowly at first and then with increasing bravery as Vincent grabbed its tip. None were close enough to aid as three additional tentacles swooped down and swept the captain upward and out of sight in mere seconds.

The Priory Five struck out immediately, allowing for no respite from the trail in their haste. For some reason, all signs were pointing toward *Mora Fenris* as the focus just as the Priory itself had been recently.

It occurred now, even as their hearts raced, that none had slept the night before and had only partaken of fragmentary meals throughout the tedious night. The early rays of the sun warmed their backs as the dust trailed behind. None halted for food or rest and very soon the confines of the prison could be seen on the horizon. At this point, Christopher slowed their pace and the group conferred.

"We should enter by the main gate," Robert suggested, pointing toward an open portal facing them.

"It does seem to be rather deserted," one of the others offered. Robert mentally identified him as Caine, testing his recall. Caine was the strongest of the group and carried the weaponry upon his steed.

"Indeed," Christopher agreed.

At this, he pointed skyward to a circling cacophony of vultures. They seemed to be vaguely watching the courtyard below.

"There!" Robert shouted, pointing excitedly. "The group's horses are wandering near the entrance!"

This visible assurance that they were following the correct path emboldened the five and no further words were spoken as they took to the trail one last time. In a few minutes, they had dismounted and joined their horses to those already grazing on the sparse vegetation surrounding the outer wall.

Each man took a longbow and shortsword from Caine's arsenal as they traversed the compromised main gate and entered the courtyard.

"There is an entrance ahead," Christopher remarked, indicating a small building near the center of the open space.

The vultures continued to call, though none made any ventures to the surface. They seemed content to wait for the time being.

Then, when the group had covered roughly half the distance between the gate and inner building, they noticed that the barren surface they trod took on a different texture and consistency. It transformed from its native density to a grainy, tenuous fiber that began to give way as they walked. Grass and vegetation disappeared within as the earth morphed and the party began to sink.

100

"What is it?" one of the group called. Robert thought it was Galen.

"The earth is turning to quicksand," Robert answered, though lacking an empirical explanation.

As the group stood ankle-deep and immobilized, something terrifying and unexpected occurred. From the depths, a pliable and organic root shot into the air and flailed about as though searching for a hold.

Lacking balance, the five attempted to arm and fire their longbows, but were unable to assault the extremity before it doubled over itself and, finding the outstretched arms of the nearest victim, wrapped around his waist, pulling him under the surface. In that instant, Caine was gone, his longbow floating atop the swirling surface.

The light from the Damascus Sword cast shadows and writhing displays upon the undulating mass of vines above. Martin, William and James stood idly, uncertain of what action to take; any projectile fired into the fray would risk hitting either Vincent or Diana and the protuberances were too distant to be reached in any other way.

Then, just as James was about to risk an adventurous volley into the roots' periphery, a foot emerged, bare and heavily grooved as though calloused from hard wear. Ankle and leg followed as Martin sheathed his sword to retrieve the errant extremities.

It was Diana, fighting and scraping against her restraints. Vincent was above, himself bound tightly by the constricting ligaments but able to pull and pry with enough authority to loosen the hold on her. Martin and William reached upward, grasping at air until Diana's feet dangled close enough, and when they did each man pulled gingerly but firmly. The vines relinquished their control on her and, just as she and her rescuers fell to the stone floor in a heap, the twisting mass redoubled its efforts and pulled Vincent upward and out of their sight.

"Vincent!" Diana shouted upward, regaining her posture again.

The vines seemed to have no interest in the escaped woman at this time, their efforts focused upon the newest prize.

Vincent thrashed and pulled at the leathery appendages, unable to gain any appreciable advantage to free himself. It was as though once relieved of its first prisoner, the entity's full attention could be focused now upon him. While it allowed him no method of escape, the arms did not seem to wish to injure or harm him. Vincent sensed that the being was searching his person for something from the manner it passingly prodded and poked.

Then, in sharp contrast to its demeanor and foretelling accuracy of Vincent's intuition, the gentle probing stopped and one of the thinner arms wrapped itself firmly around his neck. Vincent's arms were held outward and it became clear that he would not be allowed to interfere any further. He could feel the bristling hairs along the surface of the sliding tentacle, but it had only secured itself to Vincent in this way to identify its prize - the silver pendant around the captain's neck.

With a deft motion, the vine pulled the chain taut and snapped it against the tightened muscles in Vincent's neck, allowing the links to slide through and away. The pointed terminus of the offending arm wrapped tightly around the silver object and carried it deeper into the interior of the being, away and above until it was out of Vincent's sight.

XVI

The writhing vines began to calm their motion just as the four below struck upon a plan. James would launch a bolt into the being's most visible surface, hoping to elicit a response of some kind. Just as he was about to fire, a pained cry of agony escaped the indeterminate mass.

"Who is it?" Diana cried out.

None could immediately identify the source. It was not Vincent, all could agree.

It was followed by another appeal and then suddenly became silent. As it did, the motion of the being halted and grew still, creating an unearthly calm that permeated the space.

"Who are you?" Diana shouted.

In reply, a man-sized extension of the being's arms shot downward and to the floor. It was a person encased within a tightly-wound network of the being's appendages.

Martin, William and James instinctively stepped between the being and Diana. The shining Damascus Sword lay between them on the earthen floor. Without knowing who was within, and what his intentions were, James stood by, trained upon the figure and ready to fire.

A thick braid of vines connected the human figure to the central mass above. It was through this link that James surmised the being was exerting its control over the individual below and he needed no prompting to fire both bolts toward this vital conduit.

A snapping sound followed by shouted expletive punctuated the ineffective offensive and the once proud and valiant crossbow fell silent to the astonished and disapproving stares of its creators. The encased being was able to understand this as an act of aggression, and began its approach to confront its assailants. In that instant of inactivity, Diana leaped forward and, grasping the fallen Damascus Sword before any could stop her, raised the fearsome blade and brought it down into and through the being's lifeline, outstretched arm, and neck as it cowered in the brand's glow.

As the severed appendages fell, the Damascus Sword shone brighter than the sun and culminated in a blinding flash that caused all present to turn away. When it ceased, Martin, William and James opened their eyes cautiously to a scene wholly vacated of the rootlike entity. The sudden darkening of the room necessitated a few moments for eyes to adjust, but when they did, careful examination by the dim light of the few torches that remained revealed Vincent lying motionless upon the floor, next to the dismembered corpse of one of the priory attendants. The commotion had disturbed a layer of dirt, revealing a stone foundation beneath the location where the brief confrontation had taken place.

Diana and the Damascus Sword were nowhere to be seen.

Christopher, Robert, Galen, and Bertrand were waist-deep in the mire when its porosity thickened and they were able to climb out expediently. Even though the newly-formed earth seemed just as ordinary as its previously unchanged environment, the four hastened to vacate the immediate vicinity and abandon their lost ally's fallen weapons for the time being.

Robert lingered a moment longer, eyes fastened on the ground as they strode away from the dormant trap as though recalling some foggy fragment of memory. Christopher noted his hesitancy and called to him from several paces distant.

"What is it?"

Robert was unshaken as he bent low and poked and prodded at the unassuming earth. "There is something. . ." he muttered to himself, "something familiar about this . . ."

Christopher and the others could not hear or comprehend his low murmuring and in a few short moments all were standing near the entrance to the underground.

"It seems that whatever force has captured Caine has taken him below the earth," Christopher announced as prelude to the party's descent.

Robert trailed a bit behind the other three, still deep in thought regarding what they had just witnessed.

Vincent opened his eyes to an all-engulfing sensation of warmth. His last recollection had been the binding grip of the vines but now their absence and lack of familiar surroundings alerted him to the reality that he had not yet rejoined the realm of his allies.

As his eyes adjusted to the congealing blur of color around him, Vincent discovered that he was standing and had firm command of his physical senses, much unlike the most recent unpleasant vision he had experienced. Outlines and vague splashes of light remained the only observable means of exploring his surroundings outside the permeating and enveloping warmth.

This was where the extent of his influence ended, however, as his eyes and ears could not separate or translate the swirling influx of sensation and he became overwhelmed. Closing his eyes and covering his ears did nothing to stem the rising chaos around him; it was around, under and within him all at once. Just as it seemed unbearable, a great flash of the most iridescent and pure green flowed around him and covered all other input. It was as though the new hue had chased away the confusing display and Vincent's eyes focused and clarity came to him.

He was standing on a grassy plain surrounded by gently rolling hills. No visible signs of civilization broke the horizon, and he did not recognize his surroundings in any geographic manner. Looking down, Vincent saw that he was clothed in civilian attire, bereft entirely of weapons, armor or supplies. The green shade cast upon all the landscape made it initially difficult to discern sky from earth and it was at this moment that Vincent realized that there was no sun, moon, or other celestial body delineating the passage of time. He felt, for all his faculties, disconnected from his physical surroundings.

He took one step forward upon the unbroken path toward the sameness that surrounded him and walked for what seemed several minutes without experiencing any transitory sensation of the passing of distance or time. Stopping after an indeterminate span of moments, Vincent looked up, down and around in all directions and could not identify his current position as having changed by any appreciable measurement.

"Hello!" he shouted, more to break the lack of stimuli than to elicit a response of any kind.

There was no echo, no reverberation, no response. Nothing other than the beating of his own heart and breath moving through his body attested to his existence in this strange place.

After a few more immeasurable seconds, Vincent adopted a new approach. If he could not advance in any direction, perhaps he could explore the construction of this odd setting. He sat upon the regular-appearing ground and attempted to sink his fingertips into the grassy carpet at his feet. He found that, for all its genuine appearance and texture, the grass and underlying sod were impenetrable beyond a cursory examination. Vincent was not even able to pull up or sever any of the natural-appearing blades of vegetation for a closer look.

At this, the captain sat back and allowed himself to recline flat on his back, looking up at the pseudo-sky and feeling the deceptively soft vegetation bend to his shape under his weight. It was only then, after he had exhausted his immediate means of exploration and resigned himself to the current situation, that a novel spark ignited within him.

Where are you? He thought.

"I am here," spoke a soft and innocent voice.

Vincent immediately understood that the sound had traversed physical distance and had emanated from a genuine person for the first time in his abstract visions. He sprang from his prone stance to confront the creator of this new experience but just as his palms thrust him upward and his eyes were about to turn to catch a glimpse of his companion, he burst back to consciousness in the lowly subterranean lair in the company of his fellow knights.

One thing stayed with him, however.

Somehow, on a level he could not comprehend, he knew the voice.

XVII

Martin, William and James greeted Christopher's party while Vincent groggily regained his senses. At once, the prone and lifeless body of their fallen ally garnered their attention and the attendant of Vale bent low to examine the unnatural scene.

Martin retold the happenings that led to their reunion, while William and James were busily rethinking and reworking the design of the double crossbow, vowing that this was to be its final iteration regardless of future valor or infamy.

"I believe that whatever force was in possession of Lord Gallock has shifted and seeks to recover the Damascus Sword," Robert concluded as Vincent rejoined them.

"It claimed Caine in that attempt," Christopher mourned.

The group, now one weaker, shared a silent moment as it was determined to exit the cavern with the body. Vincent was preoccupied between the meaning of his most recent vision, loss of Diana and the Damascus Sword and, as his hand reached into his tunic, the puzzling theft of his pendant. He realized that the men were looking to him for guidance, and he would have to plot a strategy that balanced what he knew he could not explain to them with the outward objectives of their remaining quest.

"Caine's body . . ." Christopher trailed, pointing downward.

The eight pulled themselves from their quiet reflection to notice that the slain body, once controlled by the same mysterious force that had overwhelmed Lord Gallock, had similarly disappeared.

She looked down upon flesh and bone hands again as for the first time. Denied the passing of time in a humbling circumstance of fate, they now pulsed and flushed with her rising humanity. Eyes and ears functioned by her own will and not through the weakened faculties of the emptied vessel at her feet.

She felt *all.*

She knew *all.*

She smiled.

The eight broke the plane of the barren landscape about them, unknowing and uncertain. The mounting losses to their party notwithstanding, several conundrums perplexed the combined efforts of the mixed group.

"Perhaps we can learn more through study at the Priory," Robert suggested.

Vincent was the last to leave the underground lair, having not only the pains of reunification and subsequent loss on his mind but also the growing sense of responsibility to his lord and homeland. They had yet to recover Lord West or learn any news pertaining to his status.

And then there was the Damascus Sword.

"That may be our best chance to learning more of these strange events," Christopher bolstered.

Vincent had before gone hours without the blade in his hand or on his person, but this was a novel sensation. A growing sense of vulnerability and trepidation was overtaking him. He had grown accustomed to the empowering and numbing effects of the blade's proximity. Now, he felt hopelessly and haplessly mortal and found himself constantly on guard to the level of paranoia.

"Yes, I concur," Martin offered, as his sideways observation of his distant captain continued unchecked. "And we can certainly shelter for the evening in the Priory if we leave now."

Not only a mental and emotional malady, Vincent determined. His body itself was succumbing to the cumulative effect. Sensation reigned where before a paralyzing and pleasant separation from the unpleasant effects of humanity had created a focus unlike any he had experienced.

"Sir," James finally cut into Vincent's preoccupation.

"Yes, and paramount shall be our resolve in recovering Lord West and Diana," the captain provided.

All were in devout agreement upon this statement from their previously recumbent leader.

William and James led the procession toward the outer gates, conversing and alternately wielding the heft of the ultimate form of the mercurial sidearm. Christopher, Robert, Galen and Bertrand congregated some distance behind them, formulating meaning from the events that they had witnessed and attempting to create connections to lore in the anticipated reunion with the full resources of the Priory. This left Vincent and Martin observing from the rearmost position and postulating their own devices.

"A force is at work ever since returning from the Holy Land," Vincent observed.

"Since you took possession of the Damascus Sword," Martin replied.

"Yes, and now that it is absent, I feel a strange . . . awakening," Vincent uncharacteristically shared.

"How so?" Martin asked as James and William reached the outer gate and made to mount their steeds.

"It is difficult to explain," Vincent countered. "While I held the blade I began to feel an inner strength, an unknown resolve that pushed me forward. Now that it is gone . . ."

"You are human," Martin concocted.

"Yes," Vincent answered, as though this one simple explanation captured the entire essence of his searching. "I feel . . . human."

"Captain!" came a call from the vanguard of the scattered party, which collected all in a moment.

James sat upon his horse, pointing forward and up.

"Vultures," Martin concluded.

"Not unlike our approach to this place," Robert added.

"Yes, but these vultures look to have discovered something," Vincent noted as several of their number dove earthward toward some point of interest hidden to the group by the terrain.

The eight hastened their preparations and were on the path quickly, taking something even as commonplace as birds of carrion as an indication of import in the supernatural mood of their mission.

As the landscape unfolded around them, and a clearer picture emerged in the clear midday sun, what most certainly seemed to be a corpse lying on the pathway could easily be identified. Martin and Vincent rode onward, chasing off the scavengers, and dismounted to investigate.

Martin looked to Vincent, as both immediately recognized the body amidst its gruesome spectacle.

"It is the old man from the galley," Vincent verbalized, leaning away from the unpleasant display deep in thought.

"It is hard to tell, but there does not seem to be a visible means of death," William offered, entering the scene.

"Indeed. He was in various states of health as he crossed our path," Martin agreed, implying natural causes.

Vincent could not reconcile the thoughts and conflict within. He certainly held no familial nor amicable connections to the deceased, but he could not shake the ominous thorn that prodded his conscience. Something had changed by the man's passing, and it eluded observation.

"You stated that this man claimed to be your father while he lived?" Robert joined the silent vigil.

Vincent nodded, standing but not taking his eyes from the decaying body. "Though my father lives and I have never before seen this man."

"Though truthfully, this man only claimed you as his son," Martin responded.

Vincent and Robert turned silently, perplexed.

"Perhaps in an informal sense?" Robert investigated.

"It did not seem so," Vincent answered, interest piqued. "Though you are correct, the man never used the word father when referring to himself, only son when addressing me."

Robert turned his attention downward.

"What is it?" Vincent prodded, having learned enough of his ally's demeanor to know when a topic of interest had claimed him.

"Possibly nothing," Robert cryptically answered. Then, looking up to his leader, "we must return to the Priory. I feel something . . . unnatural . . . has happened."

Vincent and Robert shared a mutual moment of understanding to the bewildered expressions of the rest of the group.

The afternoon passed in silence as eight mounted figures flew across the trail sparing neither rest nor respite until the goal be reached. Vincent took the lead position unaccompanied to set the harried pace while others trailed in scattered formation. Very soon, the village of Westford could be seen upon the horizon and, though it lay not on the direct path to the Priory, Vincent momentarily considered a brief pause there. The child Stephanie had impressed herself upon his psyche in an indelible and indescribable manner.

With the sun again on their backs, this time on the return journey from *Mora Fenris*, Gallock's deserted camp enticed the group's curiosity but only for a moment until the Priory crested the horizon and the pace quickened for the final stretch.

"None too soon," Robert observed, as a storm of some magnitude seemed to be gathering upon their approach.

The eight tethered and secured the animals in the Priory stables and wasted no time upon breaching the main doors and storming the premises as an invading army just as distant rumbles of thunder reverberated throughout the countryside.

Robert and Christopher led the procession downward and into the caverns. There, as had been left in the not so distant past, were the scattered and collected papers and documents that had led them to the defunct prison and beckoned them back again just as swiftly.

"I know what I'm looking for . . ." Robert trailed, leaving the group and bypassing the patchwork map that remained strewed about the floor. Vincent marveled at the display, as did the others who were not present for its construction and traced the coastline and familiar environments depicted.

Christopher, Bertrand and Galen set about checking and preparing the grounds for the increasing squall that began to surround them. In the absence of several of the Priory attendants, James and William volunteered their services to the grateful remaining caretakers and as they left the scene, Martin and Vincent attempted to aid Robert in whatever way possible.

"I am in possession of a partial tome on loan from the Templars who headquartered in the Holy Land," Robert explained, producing a leather pouch with an embossed image of two knights riding a single horse. "As you know many made fortune on the sale of antiquities and relics, and the legend of the *Paladin* and artifacts connected to it are in high regard."

"It seems there is at least some truth to the legends," Martin supplied.

"Yes, without some basis of reality most would discount these as fables, but one thing caught my attention recently . . ." Robert answered, opening and carefully scanning the various items in the leather case.

"The storm grows," Vincent mused, as a particularly violent peal of thunder pierced the air and shook the ground around them.

"This," Robert cried, sliding a magnificently illuminated scrap of artwork forth.

Upon the aged and tattered parchment, Martin and Vincent beheld a scene too uncanny to be a coincidence. Lying lifeless upon a barren scene was a derelict old man, face frozen in terror at some point in the distance. Robert was continuing his search as the two knights of Ballecetine looked to each other in a mixture of apprehension and disbelief.

"This is its companion," Robert spoke, producing the other half of the masterful depiction.

The complete work caused Vincent's pulse to quicken. There, standing over and triumphant, was a life-like representation of the very silver dragon pendant which had recently been stripped from his person, only this likeness was not static nor still. It was alive and poised to strike down the prone man with spear-like talons and bared teeth.

"The words below," Martin pointed out.

Two words in Latin stood in contrast to the fearsome scene. *Adventus Axis.*

XVIII

Due to the delicate nature of the various manuscripts and artifacts housed within the Priory, the attendants would routinely secure the access points from the outside against hazards of nature when inclement weather threatened. Bertrand and Galen assigned William and James the windows and entrances on the ground level, while they and Christopher ascended to the hatches that allowed access to the upper levels and rooftops.

As they worked expediently, those native to the Priory suspected and recognized that this was an altogether unique sort of storm and its value as an omen was not lost upon them. This, together with the rapidly accumulating torrents of precipitation and raucous thunder, accelerated their efforts greatly.

William and James were thrown about as they traversed the perimeter of the main keep. Christopher had directed them to focus their efforts upon the main building, but as they worked, James saw an outbuilding near the stables that had been left unsecured. He braved the winds and driving rain to traverse the courtyard toward it.

"Where are you going?" William shouted into the storm. "There's nothing important in the stable!"

William's words were drowned out by the nearly constant thunder blasts around them. What concerned him the most, however, was the increasing ferocity of the winds. Several times, James was swept away and required a few moments to regain his bearings. William cursed his friend's tenacity and struck out as directly as possible to either intercept his wayward ally or discover what was so important as to endanger both of them.

Then, in the flash of a lightning bolt, William understood what had attracted his perceptive friend's attention. In one of the outbuildings a light flickerèd from within. This could be a major liability, William concluded, as a lit lantern in the midst of the feed and tackle for the nearby horses could easily become dislodged and start a blaze. He inwardly forgave the archer knight's assumed folly and made for the building, tracking truer than James' wandering pathway and reaching the threshold first.

When he opened the door, it flung wildly and broke from its hinges in a great gust. William stood for a moment, attempting to assess the situation, while James caught up and entered without caution. As he strode brashly through, he halted just as quickly as William had when he allowed his eyes to adjust and take in what lay before them. The source of the flickering light was not a carelessly left flame, but a source of immeasurably more worth, power and danger. Lying in repose and partially obscured in a thatch of hay was the glowing Damascus Sword.

Christopher made for the upper levels of the keep, while Bertrand and Galen secured the middle levels. Guided by frequent lightning strikes, the work was simple, though the creaking and swaying of the building in the gale was disconcerting.

At one point, Christopher climbed the ladder that he had hundreds of times before to access the roof, but found that the panel had become jammed and was allowing a great quantity of rainwater to gush down the gangway and into the keep. He pounded upon the lower surface of the large plank but it would not budge enough for him to square it in its proper alignment to stem the flow.

Galen and Bertrand appeared on the scene momentarily and realized the situation. As they made to help Christopher, he gave one last drenching shove upward, which was just enough to dislodge the cover and catch the wind. It swung upward and slammed hard against its hinges, flapping madly in the swirling storm.

A deluge of floodwaters washed down the ladder, but Christopher held firm and pulled himself up to the roof level, followed by equally soaked helpers. The wind was enough to cast them off balance initially, and as he regained his posture, Galen shouted something incomprehensible in the chaos and pointed toward the opposite end of the roof.

Through the sheets of sideways rain and blinding flashes, a person stood in opposition to the elements.

Christopher cast a confused expression toward his compatriots, who realized as well as he that the person standing before them was not only wholly unaffected by the rising power of the storm but seemed to be enraptured by it.

Casting aside the immediate work of securing the roof hatch, the three men braced against the storm and approached the figure. Speech was impossible as well as pointless, the three soon realized, as the figure turned to face them as though expecting visitors.

It was a woman, tall and clothed in a robe the color of flame that obscured all but face and hands. The pleats and edges of her attire did not succumb to the wind or the water, holding perfectly to her contours as she approached. Without speaking a word, she conveyed supreme command as not a strand of the intense midnight that flowed past her neck and shoulders strayed from its place. She looked over each of the three men who stared with bewildered and stunned disbelief.

"Your mind contains nothing of value to me," she coldly assessed, looking into and through Galen. Then, a blinding stroke of lightning lanced from the sky, incinerating him with only a momentary cry of anguish.

The proximity and intensity of the strike threw both Christopher and Bertrand backward, temporarily deaf and blind in sensory shock. Christopher felt the heat from the blast upon his face and neck; only the coldness of the pelting rain reminded him he still lived.

"We have to find a way to carry it," William announced, as James began rummaging through the building for some sort of covering or blanket.

William walked up to the blade as James continued to search. It was glowing brightly, which he knew to be a sign of some importance. Just as he was about to turn to join James in the search, a deafening peal of thunder shook the ground.

"That was a very close strike," William pronounced.

After a momentary pause, both he and James took up the search again, needing no light other than the vibrant Damascus Sword to guide them.

"What. . . have you done?" Christopher attempted to shout, "Who are you?"

It was no use. By now, the winds had accelerated to such a degree that his words were swallowed entirely by the storm as soon as they left his mouth.

The woman next walked up to a cowering and disoriented Bertrand, who had fallen next to the outer wall, covering his ears and staring blankly. He had been looking directly at his ally when the lightning had struck and could, mercifully, hear or see nothing.

"You also possess nothing I require," she stated. Christopher was somehow able to hear her clearly amid the elements and it was at that point that he realized she was not speaking at all. Her words imprinted directly into his mind.

The soon to be final member of the Priory covered his ears and attempted to protect what sensory functions he still commanded as the lethal stroke from above flashed and he alone remained to face the deadly woman's ire.

"Here," James supplied, having found a sturdy horse blanket nearby. Together, the two men covered the entire length of the blade and then carried it aloft. Even wrapped in several layers of the thick fabric, it was possible to hold the blade only for a few moments until the initial waves of debilitating cold began to flow through it. For this reason, they formed a hand-off routine. James held the package at first and, after a few moments when he felt the coldness penetrate the layers, he handed it off to William. They proceeded in this way quite effectively and exited the outbuilding to a violent rush.

The rain had subsided to a great degree, but it was the unpredictable winds that shoved and pushed the two men off course. In the intermittent flashes of lightning, a horrifying outline emerged. James and William saw it and hastened their progress as best they could as an enormous whirlwind approached, destined to make the Priory its target.

"We must get to the caverns before the Priory is destroyed!" William shouted futilely into the wind.

As his statement was torn from his mouth, a second imminent lightning strike shattered the scene, sending both James and William to the ground and the Damascus Sword skittering away and into the mud.

Christopher wandered through oblivion. This second blast had numbed all his senses except for the intense burning now doubled upon his flesh. He felt the wind buffeting him about but could see or hear nothing in the confusion. Then, the sensation of rising overtook all. He was being lifted up but not by any natural or physical means. His body floated impossibly above the soaked planks below and all outer stimuli ceased. A whisper invaded his mind.

You have use.

He attempted to form a response but had no control over his faculties. Christopher was entirely and hopelessly at the mercy of the unknown murderer of his allies.

You will live.

His eyes were open but nothing registered. He felt no cold, warmth, wet or dry. His burns disappeared and Christopher understood at that moment that he was being held not out of failure of his senses but by the will of the woman. She allowed him the pleasure of one form of sensation, opening his eyes to his surroundings. He was levitating above the roof several feet, enough to take in the remains of his charred allies, and the approach of a terrible whirlwind.

She was there as well. Her face was at arm's length, so if there were a time to strike, it was now. His limbs refused to obey his mind's decree. She was staring into and through him, indescribably.

She was . . . beautiful.

By now, the approaching roar of the whirlwind had overridden all. James and William scrambled and retrieved the bundle, finding the entrance to the Priory and entering just as pieces of the very outbuildings they had left began to disintegrate and become airborne. All depended on reaching the caverns before the entire building collapsed upon them.

Christopher felt a euphoric aura overtake him. He was viewing events as a bystander and not a participant. His body floating inexplicably, the lone attendant of Vale stared into the face of death and was entranced. Her lips moved in speech, demure and direct. His mind melted away and if this were his parting from sanity, he welcomed it wholly.

"You will know the time," she said.

Christopher was attempting to construct a verbal response but even his voice was not his own. Behind her, a massive whirlwind began tearing apart the structure he had called home his entire life. As long as he focused upon her eyes . . . the eyes . . . he was uncaring . . . the eyes.

"Who . . . are . . . you . . ." he was allowed to mumble.

She chose to speak into his mind this time, though it was the eyes . . . that spoke to him. He had seen the eyes before. They were clarity and innocence, they were so . . . green.

I am death and I am life
I seek out and I find
To know me is to be mine
I am Downfallen from all time.

Christopher felt himself losing grasp on even his consciousness. Her eyes . . .

She leaned inward and spoke into his ear, her breath cold.

"I am Axis, the Destroyer."

XIX

As soon as the words left her mouth, Axis disappeared and Christopher was thrust back into the world of chaos. His senses were at full attention and no evidence of his secondary injuries remained from the lightning strikes.

With no time to lament the remains of his final fellow attendants, the lone caretaker rushed to the open hatch and careened recklessly downward as part of the structure around him began to crumble and fly apart. The howling of the whirlwind filled all; he only hoped that those he had dispatched to other areas of the grounds had fared better than his party.

Vincent, Martin and Robert cast their attention upward as several concussive blows fell, shaking even their position deep below the earth.

"Shall we go and help the others?" Robert suggested, setting down a stack of illuminated documents.

"Stay here with the artifacts," Vincent directed. "Martin and I will investigate."

The two began ascending the staircase toward the iron door that separated them from the world above.

"This storm seems to have intensified greatly," Martin commented.

"Yes," Vincent agreed. "This is a very strange and unnatural storm." The captain felt trepidation as they reached arm's length of the door, for without the emboldening presence of the Damascus

Sword his mortality had become magnified a thousandfold. He had battled on sea and plain countless times before knowledge of the Damascus Sword's power, but now that he had tasted it, everything else fell short and wanting. He would have to retrain himself, and that process began with his hand touching the cold metal barrier before them.

"Hurry to the staircase!" William shouted as they traversed the great hall, tossing the increasingly bitter parcel to his ally.

As they ran across the shifting surface, a great crash accompanied the wall to their left falling inward and onto their path. The entire structure above them buckled, and a man emerged from the access flight to the upper levels, a river of debris and wreckage on his heels.

"Get to the caverns!" Christopher shouted.

James and William tore through the hall, aware of the absence of Christopher's two helpers but unable to communicate in any way due to the rising din. The lone attendant followed the two down the narrow staircase to the sickening background of splintering and shattering above and around them. The Priory was being ripped apart plank by plank as though found wanting by the one who had pronounced judgment on Bertrand and Galen. Christopher wondered if Axis had summoned this storm exclusively in her anger.

The three entered the access hallway that terminated in the iron door just as it opened from the inside and together all five men tumbled onto the staircase leading into the cavern in a heap. Vincent and Martin absorbed the brunt of the rush and just as Christopher cleared the threshold the entire hallway behind them crashed downward, into and through the open door.

The wrapped Damascus Sword rebounded precariously and as the covering unfurled in its descent the blade's luminescent presence made itself known. It came to rest near Robert's feet and as the five righted themselves and the dust began to settle, Vincent descended the flight and reached downward.

William and James turned to speculate on the state of the only known entrance or exit to the cavern, which was now blocked entirely by wood and foundational stone from the Priory's base. The iron door itself and surrounding frame had been cast aside and crushed, creating only an impenetrably dense wall of debris in its place.

Robert and Vincent gathered around the blade, neither touching it.

"Where did you find it?" Vincent gasped.

Christopher had collapsed against the wreckage, unknowing how he had survived his encounter and simultaneously uncertain of its meaning. Reality rushed in all around him. He knew so much that must be shared but had no words.

"It was in the stable outbuilding," James supplied after he and William had concluded that exit through the same means as their entry would be impossible.

Robert and Vincent exchanged confused glances.

"I thought you said the sword disappeared with Diana after slaying the vines?" Robert inquired.

"It did," Vincent replied, drawing the next logical conclusion. If the sword had been found, then what did that mean about Diana? Or Lord West, whose location had yet to be discovered?

"Somehow it was transported here," Robert mused out loud, rising and pacing toward his tome. "Why here? And what of Diana?"

"Captain," William interrupted, "There is no way out."

The gravity of the situation fell upon the six. Having survived the supernatural storm, and encounter with Axis, the mere questions of necessity bore into them. All eyes turned to Christopher, the only remaining individual with intimate knowledge of their location.

"I . . . saw . . . her," he mumbled.

Robert turned as Vincent came to Christopher's side.

"Who did you see?" the Captain prodded.

Christopher's mind raced to describe and express everything. It was incomprehensible. There was no way.

Robert retrieved the illuminated manuscript that he and Vincent had been studying and showed it to Christopher, who reacted immediately.

"Axis," he nearly shouted. "She was on the roof. Galen and Bertrand . . . she killed them without a thought . . ."

Robert's eyes widened as he looked down at the terrible imagery of the artwork. William and James looked to Robert, Christopher and Vincent in succession for some sort of explanation.

"She is looking for something," Christopher posited.

"She?" Vincent asked, grimacing.

Robert closed his eyes.

"Who is Axis?" James finally demanded.

Christopher's heart was still racing. Catching his breath momentarily, he was able to focus. Vincent bent down and raised the blinding Damascus Sword.

"Axis is the power we have been fighting all this time," he supplied.

"Taking the forms most advantageous to gain access to the Damascus Sword," Robert continued, eyes still closed.

"We destroyed Lord Gallock, and the vine entity in *Mora Fenris*, but all along we have only been chasing the outer signs of Axis' true power," Vincent explained, feeling complete again as the once crippling coldness of the Damascus Sword crept through his arm.

"Yes, that is accurate," Robert concurred. "We should learn what we can of this and how we can predict the next move."

"We can only stay here so long," James suggested, pushing against the unmoving wall of stone and wood that now imprisoned them.

A moment of silence fell over the group. The Damascus Sword cast the brightest light throughout the entire cavern, a light that it had maintained all the while from the outbuilding until its reunion with its bearer.

"Axis must still be here," Vincent said, holding up the sword as evidence.

"She disappeared just before the whirlwind destroyed the Priory," Christopher responded.

Robert and Vincent looked to each other.

"It is shining with the same intensity as the other moments we were in the presence of one of Axis' forms," Vincent retorted.

Robert was deep in thought.

Vincent walked to the floor of the cavern, noting how the blade's brilliance did not waver nor weaken as he traversed the perimeter of their domicile. There was no way to predict a direction or bearing; the sword simply shone its light with intensity regardless of his position.

Distant rumbling of thunder sounded above, and rivulets of the deluge seeped into the cracks and down the steps. Christopher moved from the site of his unceremonious landing moments before and joined Vincent upon the floor level.

James, William and Martin continued to investigate the doorframe and surrounding foundation. Using various implements, levers, and tools at their disposal, they were unable to gain any appreciable ground removing the blockage. Robert retreated to his collected information, confounded and yet at the brink of discovery. He had the faintest recollections and memories that came from his general studies while abroad but more remained to be learned before he put forth any worthwhile observations of his own.

Christopher joined the Captain, both staring into the lustrous pattern of the Damascus steel. It was entrancing. Could it be as simple as Axis sought the blade? That was certainly her focus while in command of Lord Gallock and his men.

"There is still something to be discovered here," Vincent declared. "A reason that the blade shines, and that you were spared."

Christopher could do nothing but agree. Truthfully, he had no words to describe his being spared by the seemingly omnipotent Axis. What he could offer eluded him entirely.

Martin, James and William returned to the lower level and joined Robert, who seemed to have found something of importance.

"This," the studious knight cried, attracting the attention of the others across the cavern.

Robert lifted a document covered from margin to margin with script. Vincent and Christopher were soon as his side and together the six looked on while Robert spoke.

"It will take some time to translate, but this is an account of Rome's excavation efforts on the fringes of the Empire."

"This place was created by the Romans," Christopher offered, each memory reminding him of what had been lost or destroyed.

"Yes," Vincent echoed, touching the thousand-year-old artifact. "Here, the name Axis is mentioned."

Christopher became preoccupied at this point and left the group. He spoke as he wandered away, "Even the Romans were seeking something in this place . . . there was something I was told, long ago, by the previous caretakers . . ."

Vincent turned his attention, handing the script back to Robert for further analysis.

"This cavern was carved by their expertise, but there was more . . ." Christopher continued.

By this time, the remainder of the group, without Robert, had gathered near Christopher at a point near the far wall of the cavern. He was running his hand along the alternately smooth and rough textures of the Roman stonework.

"If the Romans were mining in this area, then perhaps this cavern was a central location for exploratory mineshafts," Martin suggested.

Christopher acknowledged Martin's words while continuing to scan the chiseled surfaces of the walls.

"Then there must be a way out from this cavern," James continued.

"Perhaps," Christopher replied. "But the mines have fallen into disrepair over hundreds of years."

"If we could find just one branch that leads to the surface," William added, expanding Christopher's search while the others did likewise.

"Finding an access point into the tunnels will be the first obstacle, assuming that they exist at all," Vincent said, looking all about for any discoloration or change in the strata surrounding them for a clue.

"Here," Martin interrupted, several paces distant from the others.

In an instant, William, Christopher, James and Vincent congregated near a thick mass of roots that had invaded a section of the wall. To the casual observer, the earthen overgrowth was simply a result of the subterranean layout of the cavern. To the men trapped within, it was an omen and suspicious oddity to the otherwise stone-faced walls.

After hacking through several intertwined woody roots that had no doubt taken many years to form, Martin began digging into earth, and then chunks of rock and loose material began to cascade downward toward his feet. James intervened, as the gap began growing and just as the two men had cleared a crevice large enough for both to stand within, Martin punched through and fell headlong into an opening on the other side. James followed, shoving aside and clearing the opening.

Even Robert was torn from his study to view the discovery.

"We will need light," Martin called back after traversing a few steps into complete darkness. "But we must be careful without knowing if there is access to fresh air."

Christopher retrieved several oil lamps and made to enter the newly formed passage, intercepted only by Vincent and the blinding Damascus Sword, which cut a path into the extent of what was visible down the corridor.

Hard-packed dirt floors attested to the volume of traffic that once trod the passage. The texture of the walls was hewn, much like the walls of the cavern, complete with clefts that still housed long expired lamps from antiquity. There was no longer any doubt; if there were to be an exit from their current predicament, it was ahead and into the darkness.

XX

Vincent and Martin struck upon the hardened path shoulder-to-shoulder with room to spare in the passageway.

"There should be a vertical shaft with access to the surface soon," Robert supplied from the rear.

William and Christopher meandered, touching and feeling the history that surrounded them with each step; the former marveling at the architecture and craftsmanship and the latter unbelieving of what lay within reach his entire lifetime.

"The air is fresh; there must be access to the surface somewhere," James supplied.

Vincent continued to wonder as to the nature of the Damascus Sword. It had maintained its light since James and William had found it. This kept him hopeful but tense as the six stepped farther and farther into the unknown.

"There," Martin pointed forward and to the left. A patch of discolored stone marked the presence of some milestone to break the sameness of their surroundings.

The six quickened their pace, reaching a smooth portion of the chiseled stone wall. It was separate in construction from the rest of the passage, very clearly having been carved from a different piece of stone and placed purposely where it stood.

"It could be an intersecting corridor," Robert posited.

"But why seal off part of the mine in such a time-consuming way?" Martin responded, certain that something of importance awaited behind.

There were no markings, hand-holds or immediately visible means of moving the slab. It spanned the entire height of the corridor and tucked behind the adjacent stone of the walls on both sides.

"This must have been placed from someone on the other side of the barrier," Robert suggested. "Otherwise there is no way it could so seamlessly fit into the opening."

"Someone who doesn't want anyone from this side to follow," Martin considered.

Martin and James pushed on the flat surface, but it was immovable. Even with the aid of all the party members, there was no way human strength could budge the barrier.

"We could get some tools from the cavern to break through," Christopher suggested.

"Let us see what other mysteries are within first," Vincent countered, following the light of the Damascus Sword into the corridor.

The six left the oddity behind for the time being, and continued straight as the light of the Damascus Sword shone the path. After a few moments, all present noticed that the blade's effect began to dull. A few steps more and those in the back of the formation had trouble navigating the darkness and all halted to form a strategy.

"We could light the lamps to continue," Robert suggested.

Vincent turned and walked through the group, noting how the blade's intensity began to grow as he retraced their route toward the mysterious barrier.

"I think that we are intended to find more to the strange wall we discovered earlier," Christopher commented inwardly claiming victory, his curiosity captured by the seamless slab.

"Indeed," Vincent whispered, leading the party back toward the Damascus Sword's focus.

Predictably, the blade's brightness continued to increase until the point that it was again difficult to look upon directly. The six found themselves at the impasse created by the smooth barrier's presence. No other avenues or straying pathways had presented themselves in the span of their travels underground thus far; if there were more to be found it seemed clear that it would be done by conventional means of lighting.

Vincent came to the forefront of the group and stood directly before the slab. The Damascus Sword pulsated in rhythm with his rising heartbeat, as though to affirm his curiosity. The captain raised the sword to eye level and held it flat against the sheer barrier, and to the shock and amazement of all, he and the Damascus Sword fell through and disappeared from the party's sight.

Martin and Robert, the closest to Vincent's position as he vanished, reached out reflexively but only met the solid, cold stone. The group looked to each other in disbelief and apprehension.

Vincent, unprepared for the lack of resistance as he reached out, stumbled and fell onto a smooth surface. The Damascus Sword initially left his grasp and slid across the glassy floor, but it quickly became secondary to his attention as his eyes took in the scene around him.

Perfectly smooth and polished stone planes intersected at the corners of the symmetrical and square room. The room reflected the light from the Damascus Sword, the only object in the closed-off space to break the darkness. There was no way that human hands could have fashioned this place, Vincent thought.

As he stood slowly, the pulsing light of the sword illuminated an etching on the wall before him. There were no objects in the perfect cube of a room and no evidence of his means of access or eventual exit. Walking toward the middle, Vincent retrieved the Damascus Sword and held it before him as he examined the image.

A winged creature, recognized by the captain as a representation of an angel from his expansive knowledge of religious icons and images in his travels, looked toward and vaguely past his position. Several details caught his immediate attention. The angel wore four red sashes around its shoulder and held a silver orb in its right hand. Upon the sashes an inscription could be read:

The four Archangels are always keen
Of he who bears dread Damascene

Vincent recognized the words at once as the inscription upon the lower half of the Damascus Sword's wooden case. Was the image before him an archangel? The recurrence of the number four caught the captain's attention. There were four sashes. Did this signify the presence of four heavenly beings?

As he contemplated these things, Vincent wished for the presence of his allies. Robert or Christopher could have enlightened him further, but there were no visible means for exit from this place to summon the others, and there were more cryptic symbolisms upon the other walls that beckoned his inquisitive mind.

The immediate consequence of Vincent's disappearance was the casting of the corridor into palpable and debilitating darkness. Christopher and Robert fumbled with the lamps in the confusion, and eventually lit one and then a second. The light provided was scant compared to the sunlike glare of the Damascus Sword, but it would have to suffice in the confines of the mineshaft.

"This is unnatural," Robert whispered, running his fingers along the ancient smooth surface, noticing that even though Vincent had just passed entirely through, the ancient dust had not been disturbed.

"There must be a way inside," Martin declared, taking one of the lamps and following their initial pathway into the darkness. James followed while the other three continued to examine the point of entry.

Moving on to his right, Vincent viewed an inscription on the wall perpendicular to the first by the light of the Damascus Sword. It was a life-like depiction of the Silver Dragon from both the illuminated manuscript in Robert's possession and the recently pilfered trinket that had formerly hung around his neck. Just as with the setting of the archangel, there was no background or other objects to form a frame of reference, but there were accompanying words near the dragon's feet:

> *Deceivers four have sworn again*
> *To plant the Seed in honored men*

This Vincent recalled from the last days of the campaign in the Holy Land. Again, the number four played a significant role. Were the deceivers somehow connected to Axis? What was the 'Seed'? He absently felt the place upon his chest where the pendant had rested all those years away only to be taken from him in a confusing moment of conflict.

Turning his focus toward the wall through which he had entered the room, Vincent saw that there was no visual representation of any kind upon its surface. This puzzled him at first, but as he stood closer to investigate, he saw that there were words only:

I am death and I am life
I seek out and I find
To know me is to be mine
I am Downfallen from all time.

Vincent reached out and traced the words as he read them aloud. There was no identifier or clue as to the speaker of the inscription or who it might describe like the others.

Stepping back toward the center of the barren room, Vincent from this perspective noticed that each of the depictions was centered on their respective surfaces, with the words either within the etching itself or very nearby. In the case of the third wall, the inscription was oddly spaced near the bottom, as though there had been an image at one time. This made no sense to him. The pictures and words all seemed to have been made at the same time though they showed no signs of wear of aging. Nothing in the room showed the worse for the passing of time, the more Vincent considered it. Not even a layer of dust covered the polished floor.

James and Martin walked at a faster pace than their initial exploratory gait. The mine tunnel continued for at least as long as the segment that connected the cavern to their first stopping point, and then another surface loomed into sight ahead in the weak light. Martin, being the first to investigate, discovered that the path terminated as it connected to another, perpendicular corridor. He stood for a moment as though considering which path to follow, then suggested a novel sentiment.

"Do you feel it strange that, if this were a mine, there are no tool marks along the walls or extraction sites?"

James pondered this oddity.

"It makes you wonder if the Romans truly were seeking wealth and materials in this place, or . . ." Martin trailed.

"Were they here not to take something *from* this place, but to leave something *behind*," James finished.

"I think we are meddling with powers that were intended to be buried and forgotten," Martin concluded.

Turning to each direction and then back toward their point of origin, the two conflicted knights stood idly in a moment of silent indecision.

Had Vincent taken the time to look closer initially, he certainly would have begun his journey at the fourth and final wall. As he walked from the oddly vacant first wall, eyes still askew toward its bland appearance, this last etching was before him before he had a chance to prepare himself for its impact.

It was Diana.

"We need to alter our thinking as to the purpose of this place," Martin spoke as he and James entered the others' sphere of vision.

"This *place* is not a *mine*," William edged, sensing that he was about to lose his prime position as originator of the notion.

At this point, all five men launched into the same dissonant accord, noting the absence of mining paraphernalia, insufficient venting rises, lack of evidence supporting the removal of ore and general paranoia surrounding the supernatural aura of the cavern.

"So, what is to be done?" Martin thundered over the assembly.

At this, all fell silent.

Vincent leaped toward the impeccable likeness. There was no doubt; the lone daughter of Lord West looked on in vague apathy toward the center of the space. His left hand flew to her face, exactly as he had remembered it for that faint moment they had caught each others' eye while in the grasp of the rootlike entity. The captain at first resolved to cast aside the Damascus Sword to lift both hands to the simple lines and shapes that represented all he had sought and lost, but then he thought better. Lifting the shining sword aloft, he pressed it to the smooth stone surface just as he had in the outer corridor to see if he could elicit a similar response.

After several seconds' contact, Vincent was about to allay his impetuous line of reasoning until the visage disappeared, leaving behind only the smooth stone of the supernaturally formed place. In the vacuum of uncertainty, Vincent stepped back unknowing if he had acted unwisely and was about to press the blade against the blank plane again when a voice sorely missed and feared lost for all time called to him from behind.

XXI

Three year's separation came to an end as Vincent and Diana embraced near the center of the silent and mysterious chamber. Overwhelming joy and relief flooded through both as each also knew and understood the seriousness of their current situation.

"There is so much," Diana pronounced between sobs, "so much I must tell you, Vincent."

"I didn't know that I would see you again," the uncharacteristically emotive captain whispered.

"When I saw you, in the vines," Diana cried, falling into his arms.

"How did you come to this place?" Vincent plied, holding her close as the Damascus Sword continued to illuminate the space brightly.

"While the vines held me fast," Diana explained, separating at arm's length and wiping her tears, "I felt a power attempting to force its way into my mind. It was seeking something."

"Yes," Vincent answered, knowing the exact sensation.

"While it probed my mind, I was able to block its power while you and your men intervened. I learned how to deceive it. To use it," she triumphantly divulged.

"When it took me I felt the same, it was as though its power had been weakened by attempting to hold both of us," Vincent added.

"When I escaped, I knew that it would only be moments before it focused its entire strength upon you," Diana explained. "When I struck it with the sword, it became angry and attempted to sweep all of us away. That was when I used its power against itself. I controlled its direction and its anger but I could not for long. It wanted the sword more than anything, and I tried to remove it and hide its location as best as I could. . ."

At this point, Diana could continue no longer and became overwhelmed.

"What is it?" Vincent asked, wiping her tears.

"I knew that my father was . . . also held by its power. It was the same power that had come to Ballecetine to imprison us. It needed us alive . . ." she broke into tears at this point.

"Where is your father, Diana?" Vincent asked directly.

She looked up through the veil of tears. "I had so little time, and I knew I could not let it know the location of the sword. I . . . lost contact with him."

Vincent held her tight as the flow of tears came unchecked now. His vision becoming obscured, he had to blink and force himself to focus several times to see a blur of motion in his periphery. He cast his vision to the right, toward the previously blank wall of his entry. Something had changed.

"We should explore the darkness ahead and find an exit to this place," James suggested.

"What of the captain?" William retorted.

"We could attempt to dig around the plate," Christopher offered. "Perhaps it could be pried or forced open if we found its edges."

"What do you make of all this?" Martin directed toward the so far silent Robert, who had been resting with his back to the smooth wall.

"I am uncertain the meaning of this," he admitted, which Martin could tell was a painful confession. "We are in the midst of a great supernatural occurrence. There can be no predicting or knowing."

This was, possibly, the greatest revelation of all. Each man had been trying to form a semblance of reality or meaning to the strange events that had been directing their actions. Unknowingly, what Robert felt a statement of resignation and powerlessness became an empowering and bolstering foundation for a renewed resolve. There was no precedent, therefore all present would be called upon to add their individual strengths to the effort in whatever capacity required.

"Then we shall do all we can to secure both our objectives," Martin stated, speaking for this new spirit. "Christopher, take William and Robert and make what preparations you can for excavating around the plate. James and I will explore deeper into the tunnels."

This was what the group needed, a firm direction and lead in the absence of the captain. Each man found a purpose and tended to it for the benefit of the group.

Martin followed Christopher back to the main cavern. "We will need a good length of rope and well-stocked oil lamps," he stated as William and Robert began searching the edges of the smooth stone wall.

"What is it?" Diana asked, pulling away as she sensed a sudden tension in Vincent's posture.

Vincent held her hand while taking the lead and walking cautiously toward the vacant wall. Diana became concerned as she watched him stare blankly ahead.

"There was writing," Vincent spoke, turning toward her but keeping his eyes fixed upon the wall. "Before I found you, there was writing . . ."

At this, Vincent left Diana's company and walked to each of the walls in succession. They were all devoid of any of the images or inscriptions that he had previously viewed.

"Vincent, what is going on?" Diana called from across the room.

He came to meet her again in the center, puzzled and confounded. "We were exploring the caverns, after the whirlwind . . ."

"Whirlwind?" Diana interrupted.

Vincent attempted to organize his thoughts. He had to reconcile his confusion with the knowledge that Diana had no understanding of the things that had recently transpired.

"Yes, after leaving *Mora Fenris*, we came to the Priory to form a strategy. It was destroyed by a whirlwind and we took shelter in a cavern below the foundation. This place is an extension of an abandoned mine that we found underground."

Diana was following the exposition while looking for an opportunity to interject.

"The Priory of Vale?" Diana shot.

Vincent halted long enough to indicate that it was so.

"Vincent, we are nowhere near the Priory of Vale," she stated in a factual manner that Vincent had to respect in silent bewilderment.

"Vincent, when I felt that I was able to manipulate the power that held us in the vines, I had but a second to choose a location to hide before the power overwhelmed me. I cast the sword down and was about to call myself and my father home to Ballecetine when I saw four great shining stars in front of me."

Vincent was enraptured and stood agape.

"I knew that the four stars were locations of power, and I knew that the force that held me was searching for that same power. I tried to send the sword, myself, and my father each to one of the stars. I did not know where it would take us, but I cast myself to the farthest star and just now awakened when you arrived here."

"So we have no idea where we are?" Vincent inquired, again holding her close.

Diana looked up into his eyes. "We could be anywhere, Vincent. I'm so sorry."

"No, no, don't be sorry . . ." Vincent trailed, less in a soothing heartfelt manner and more in a moment of absent discovery.

"What is it?" Diana asked.

"Four points of power. . ." he trailed.

"Yes, they were shining like stars," Diana reiterated.

Vincent turned away, deep in thought. "While in the caverns below the Priory, we were investigating an artifact that we believed to hold answers to the strange things that were happening. A tapestry decorated with various locations caught our attention and was a vital clue in our finding you at *Mora Fenris*. There were four locations depicted on the tapestry."

"Four stars," Diana whispered.

"Four stars," Vincent echoed.

"What were the locations?" Diana asked, instantly curious.

"Some were unknown to us at the time. The central location was the Priory itself. We determined another to be the abandoned prison *Mora Fenris*, where we found you," Vincent explained.

"Other than that, another showed a graveyard, and the fourth was a tall stone tower of unknown origin."

"I wonder if those locations were the stars that I saw?"

"It is very possible," Vincent answered. He was purposely hiding the fifth element of the tapestry and, though time and distance had separated the two of them previously, Diana knew at once that there was more.

"What else was shown on the tapestry?" She prodded.

"There was another symbol, toward the bottom of the artifact," Vincent divulged. "It was a crusader cross, entwined with the image of the silver dragon that you gave me before I left."

Diana was confused by this at first. Vincent raised his eyes to meet hers.

"The silver dragon pendant was taken by the vines while I was in their grasp and disappeared with it when you left."

Martin and James ventured out upon the same route they had already trod, stopping at the intersection where the first path stopped and branched into two.

"We will leave a rope trail behind as we search each pathway," Martin explained, setting one end on the ground and taking the remaining coil in his hand.

Choosing the left, the two men warily walked into the darkness.

Robert, Christopher, and William began chipping away at the stone surrounding the smooth door. Initially, William suggested using the tools to simply break through the barrier, but several blows and bent tools attested to the superior strength of the unknown material.

Just as Martin's and James' lanterns disappeared from view into the dark pathway, Robert dislodged a large piece of sediment, causing a small trail of dust and rock to settle at their feet. At this, the three paused momentarily, looking to the stable-appearing ceiling and judging the distance to the security of the cavern.

"I think we should be fine," William answered the unasked question and continued chiseling.

The corridor was remarkable in its endless sameness. Inwardly, Martin wondered how far from the Priory proper they had wandered below ground. Certainly, they were far from the foundations of the buildings by now. If there were a way to simply ascend directly upward via any sort of foothold or tunnel, they would be in the vast countryside.

"There must be an exit, the air in the tunnels moves," James commented, standing still and observing the flickering nature of the lamp's flame.

By this time, they had exhausted half of the rope's length. With the intersection behind them a distant memory, the two bravely journeyed onward.

Stopping periodically to gauge their progress, the three impromptu miners could tell that they were getting close. A clearly defined edge could now be identified around the smooth door.

"Let's each pry on the sides and maybe we can pull it out," William suggested while the group situated themselves for one last, definitive end to the mystery of the hidden room.

Robert and William jammed their chisels behind one side while Christopher applied leverage to the other.

"On three," William announced.

They stood prepared and tensed.

"One, two . . . three!" he shouted and the three diverted all their might and body weight into the endeavor.

"It's moving!" Christopher grunted.

"Keep going!" Robert encouraged, as groans and snapping sounds became audible from behind the door.

In their last burst of energy, the three felt their chisels slide behind the smoothness of the panel and it jarred free, falling over and crashing onto the hard-packed pathway between them without breaking.

They dropped their tools to rush into the room but were confounded. William and Robert looked to each other and then to Christopher, who had no explanation.

Behind the 'door' was nothing but solid rock.

XXII

"We should tell James and Martin," Christopher muttered, not taking his eyes from the confusing discovery.

William physically examined every inch of the exposed rock and dirt behind the door. There were no supernatural or ordinary clues that anything unusual had occurred.

Robert left, lantern in hand, to rejoin the two exploring the tunnel, uncertain of how he would explain their find.

Christopher moved his analysis to the fallen stone panel. William had progressed to removing material around the edges of the newly-created doorway.

"Perhaps it is not the physical space, but this strange object that is the key," Christopher spoke mostly to himself but audibly enough that it caught William's attention.

"We should take it back to the cavern," William suggested, stopping his menial work and bending down to the ground next to Christopher.

It was too heavy for the two of them, so Christopher and William waited for the return of the others.

Finding the rope in the near darkness, Robert walked hunched over with his lantern trained upon the ground and attention only partially on the path. In a few moments, he heard voices from ahead and saw the doubly powerful glow of two lanterns.

"Come quickly," Robert called, waving his lantern over his head to attract attention.

Martin and James abandoned the rope and came with all possible haste given the terrain and darkness.

"What is it?" Martin demanded as the three reunited.

"The stone. . ." Robert began but lacked the words to express something he could not explain.

"Let's go," Martin decided, leading the trio back toward the first intersection and then quickly to the excavation site.

"What is it?" Martin asked, observing the situation and implied confusion.

James immediately began scrutinizing the earth behind the stone plate's previous location, dumbfounded.

"We don't know what this means," Christopher spoke the only words that could be truthfully uttered.

Martin looked to Robert, who had nothing more to offer and then to William, who simply shook his head. The group had come to an impossible situation, and for the first time Martin did not know what to say or do to raise their morale.

"We would like to take the stone plate back into the cavern and investigate it further," Robert offered in the growing silence.

"Very well," Martin complied, and four of them lifted the stone, which was considerably weighty, while Robert led them back toward the cavern with all the lanterns.

Robert constructed a makeshift stand out of some of the heavier wooden fixtures in the cavern, and the men carefully set the tall rectangular stone on its edge so that it stood in roughly the same attitude as it had in the corridor and they could examine all its surfaces.

Robert and Christopher traced the edges of the magnificent carving, noting how there was no residue clinging to its surface from the dirt and grime of centuries of silent solitary existence.

"It is entirely seamless and carved expertly," William noted as he regarded the stone.

The lines were perfectly square, and its color and texture were uniform. No one present had ever seen anything like it.

"Learn what you can while we make preparations for an earnest expedition into the tunnels," Martin coaxed. "There is evidence that the passages do lead to the outside if we can only reach their end."

With this, Robert and Christopher pulled themselves from the observable and unexplainable to the less abstract but yet cryptic contents of their combined accumulation of relics and documents. James seemed willing enough to abandon anything involving the caverns and joined Martin in collecting supplies, while William engaged himself in a deeper examination of the cavern's walls and environment, satiating his own brand of curiosity.

"What does this power want with the silver dragon?" Diana inquired.

"I feel it is much the same connection as to the Damascus Sword," Vincent replied, holding the bright blade up to observe its pulsating glow.

Both he and Diana stood silent for a moment until Diana ventured a brave hand to touch the silver hilt. Initially, Vincent felt the urge to stop her, but then allowed his curiosity to take over, as he remembered from the others' retelling of events that Diana had wielded the blade with no ill effects.

"It is. . . cold," she whispered, running her fingers along the smooth metal.

Vincent held the sword out, inviting her to hold it to witness the evidence for himself. As she took the handle firmly in both hands, the pulsating rhythm of the brightness changed. Vincent understood that it had imprinted Diana's rapidly increasing heartbeat onto itself, and had left behind his own relatively calm pulse. As this occurred, Diana began to falter, as though losing consciousness.

"Steady," Vincent called out, reaching out to hold her, but refraining from reclaiming the weapon.

"I feel . . . dizzy," Diana whispered, beginning to fade out of consciousness. "It is the same as . . . in the . . . prison. . ."

At that moment, Vincent saw that her knees began to buckle and he instinctively pulled her close to him just as a familiar sensation overtook his senses and both of them fell into darkness.

It was akin to the visions that he had experienced, though in this particular occurrence he did not feel the same passing into or out of consciousness that had accompanied the others. Diana, however, had become dead weight and slumped into his embrace.

As the world around them rematerialized, it was to a horrific panorama of weightless floating. Everything was darkness, except four distant and pulsating points of light. Vincent could not draw a breath to speak or rouse Diana and began to feel a growing force repelling them from each other.

Wrapping both arms securely around her dormant frame, Vincent gripped the handle of the Damascus Sword with both hands and used it as an anchor as the force grew in might. They were indeterminately drifting toward one of the four starlike lights, and Vincent felt deep within that these were locations corresponding to the tapestry, but there was no way to decipher which star corresponded to which location. Experiencing the effect for himself, Vincent could now appreciate Diana's sense of loss upon losing contact with her father; it was becoming increasingly difficult to keep her next to him.

The slightest quiver of motion alerted him to Diana's waking. Her initial fear followed by expression of familiarity reassured Vincent that this was the same effect she had experienced after the confrontation in the prison.

Diana raised her hands to his, but it was to strengthen her hold on the Damascus Sword. Vincent found that as long as both of them held fast to the blade, and concerned themselves less with holding to each other, the repelling force subsided significantly.

With this knowledge, the pair were able to wend their pathway toward the stars by simply directing the Damascus Sword toward them. Propulsion was inexplicable, and neither sensed the need for air nor speech in this place; the longer they stayed the closer their minds began to grow.

Upon approaching, Vincent and Diana witnessed the four stars pulsing with the combined frequency of the Damascus Sword's glow. Since neither knew which point would be more advantageous than another, and the pace of their acceleration was increasing now, Vincent felt Diana direct the blade toward the closest point. He added his resolve to hers and felt the sensation of increasing speed, even though there was no semblance of air or landscape by which to judge such a concrete experience, and the bright point of light became an all-consuming sun before its explosion in a bright flash of pure light.

Martin and James were traversing the various cloisters dotting the edges of the cavern while a great resounding crash filled the entire space.   Robert and Christopher came running immediately and William ignored all else as he rushed to the propped stone slab.

Vincent and Diana had fallen through the door, much as Vincent had disappeared into it earlier, coming to rest in an exhausted heap upon the floor, each gasping for breath as though drowned. William, having been vaguely looking in that direction, was the only one to have witnessed the effect, but he noticed that something was wrong immediately.

"Where. . . are we?" Diana gasped, still breathing heavily and too weak to rise.

"You are in the caverns beneath the Priory," James offered as all five had now gathered and exchanged uncertain looks.

Vincent raised himself to a crouch, feeling his facial features as his lungs filled again as though they had forgotten how to function, and recoiled immediately.   A beard of several week's growth had sprung forth inexplicably and, as he took in the sight of his long-lost one, Vincent detected lines and streaks of silver invading the dark locks of her youthful features.

Diana rose to meet Vincent's posture and each looked on the other in disbelief, though this seemed superficial to the onlooking stares of their reunited allies.

XXIII

Vincent rose slowly, looking about the cavern. The stone plate stood before him, displaced from its original location. This made sense now, as he understood it to be the junction between this world and the strange place he and Diana had just left.

"Where were you?" Martin inquired for the group's stunned silence.

"Honestly, I can't say for certain," Vincent replied, scratching at his wiry facial hair in annoyance.

"Time passes differently while in the other world," Diana observed, touching his face. "We must be careful how long we stay."

Robert and Christopher examined the stone plate, which had not changed in any way other than a minute shifting in position from the force of Vincent and Diana's reappearance.

"Other world?" James echoed.

Vincent and Diana spent the next several minutes recounting the details of the time between Diana's disappearance in the underground to the present. Vincent spoke also to the notion that the stone plate was a doorway into the vacant room where he had discovered Diana.

"Where else do these doorways lead?" Robert inquired.

"I believe that they correspond to the locations on the tapestry," Vincent announced. "One terminus is here, in the caverns beneath the Priory."

Christopher was deep in thought, saying nothing as the others began to converse.

"The other location that we know is *Mora Fenris*," Robert connected.

"How was it that you and the sword disappeared in that place?" James asked Diana.

"I am not certain, but knowing what we know now about the operation of the stone doorway, I feel it is possible that we were standing *upon* one of them and Diana fell through it as she grasped the Damascus Sword," Vincent explained, then turned toward her, "she is the only one who seems capable of accessing the four stars that connect the locations."

This revelation did spark interest in Robert's mind.

"Diana cannot only *touch* but *wield* the Damascus Sword," Martin trailed.

"I cannot explain it," Vincent continued.

Diana endured the group's scrutiny. She could detect curiosity and an undercurrent of distrust among the gathering.

"All I can say for certain is that we were fortunate to find our way back here," Vincent expounded. "It is very confusing to navigate the space between the doors. Diana proved instrumental in that regard."

Robert was intrigued, noticing how the Damascus Sword continued to pulsate brightly before them. "Perhaps it is the proximity to the stone door that causes the blade to glow," he posited.

Christopher remained silent, running his hand along the smooth edges of the portal. "For generations, those who have lived and worked here have felt an unknown and strange power."

All turned to face the lone attendant of Vale.

"This is no happenstance that has caused us to meet here, and the dangers and losses that have been felt. We must learn all that we can about this power. The presence of Axis within our world demands it. We can ignore it no longer."

The group gave its nonverbal assent as Christopher spoke, each knowing the losses to which he referred. Diana especially felt a pang of grief, having been unknowingly responsible for the death of one of their number.

"Before, I simply held the sword up to the door and I fell through," Vincent added.

"That was the feeling I experienced in the underground prison as well," Diana concurred. "I was holding the sword and the next moment I was falling until I released the sword."

"And it was then that you became imprisoned within the wall of the empty room?" Robert edged, still attempting to learn the mysteries they had witnessed.

"Yes, but it felt all as one moment," Diana explained. "The moment I lost the sword, losing contact with my father, appearing in the room with Vincent. I had no knowledge of the passing of time."

"You had no knowledge that you were imprinted upon the wall," Vincent added.

Diana nodded.

"We are not only dealing with dangers of the supernatural but also the passing of time itself," Robert mused.

"I wonder. . ." James muttered.

"Yes, what is it?" Martin plied, who was the closest to the inquisitive knight's side. "We must explore all options and notions."

James seemed unwilling to take the lead in the discussion but stepped forward nonetheless. "Is it possible for others to enter the doorway? Could we find the other locations from the tapestry?"

This was a novel thought, though not wholly unexplored in Robert's and Christopher's minds. Christopher looked to be about to speak when Robert took the initiative.

"We still do not understand the nature of the connection," Robert pointed out. "It seems that in Diana's situation she was transported directly to the 'four stars' as you described it. But when Vincent fell through the door in the passageway he was taken to the empty room."

"Both situations have one commonality," Christopher edged.

All looked to him, as he walked among the group and halted near Diana.

"In both situations, the sword seeks out Diana."

The others hadn't thought of it that way before, but Christopher had a valid point.

"So, what would happen," James countered, "if Diana were to travel through the doorway?"

The object of their discussion became uneasy as the strategy seemed to focus upon her more and more directly.

"Our first goal should be the safe exit from here," Martin redirected. "Until we can get a clear picture of the state of matters outside this place we will be no closer to unraveling the mysteries around us."

"Very true," Vincent commended, walking to the stone door and noting that while he did not have the Damascus Sword in his grasp it was just as solid as its appearance would suggest. "What have your expeditions revealed as to the nature of the passages?"

Martin grimaced in disgust. "There is no clear exit, though we have not explored the extent of the tunnels. Perhaps now that you are here, and the sword. . ."

"Yes, we should endeavor to find a natural exit from here before exploring things we do not yet understand," Vincent concurred, following his most trusted ally's line of reasoning in the most sublime nature that only they understood.

The seven sprang to action, Martin and James disbursing oil lamps while Robert and Christopher complied and stowed away the scattered documents and papers from their recent explorations. If this foray were successful, they might not return to the cavern for some time.

In short order, the group proceeded to enter the tunnels. With Vincent and Martin at the forefront, the light from the Damascus Sword lit the way exceptionally until they approached the site of the stone door's discovery. Vincent paused, examining the excavated site in wonder, and turned to face the group.

"As suspected, the sword glows in response to the presence of the stone door," he announced, the waning light a clear testament. "We will need to use lamps from this point onward."

William and James were at the rear of the procession and took one last look toward the cavern that they both hoped would soon become a memory.

Diana, Christopher and Robert followed in the middle, though they were also the most curious among the group and often lagged behind the pace set by the pair in front, Vincent on the right and Martin on the left. Soon, the group came to the intersection where Martin had begun laying the rope to mark their progress. By this time, the Damascus Sword had resumed its plain appearance, and for this reason Vincent stashed it through his belt to observe the walls and ceiling of the tunnels as they walked.

"There certainly is an exit to the outside," Vincent remarked. "The air is too fresh to have been sealed off for centuries."

Martin concurred. "We are also of the opinion that the use of these passages as mines is suspect."

Vincent nodded. "I agree, there is no evidence that anything was ever taken from here. It seems as though these were escape tunnels or possibly access tunnels for the construction project of the cavern."

"Should we all explore the same pathway?" Martin inquired as the seven stood at the crossroad.

"Perhaps that would be advisable," Vincent answered. "At least until we reach the end of the rope."

In the increased light of several lamps this time, the party was able to see the entire outline of the floor, walls and ceiling. They followed Martin and James' initial pathway until the rope terminated in the pile that Martin had abandoned when called back to the cavern.

"This is the extent of our exploration," Martin announced, and the group took a brief pause to confer.

"Let's take this pathway as far as the rope will take us," Vincent decided. "Then we can assess our progress."

Martin took up the coiled rope and continued the trail. There was no indication of an exit ahead, though it was James who pointed out something of interest.

"A faint light, do you see it?" he nearly shouted, becoming quite excited at the prospect of daylight.

"Yes," Vincent squinted and the group picked up the pace.

They came closer and closer, and the rope shortened in Martin's grasp. There was another side corridor, beaming a weak light onto the dirt floor ahead. Upon reaching it, Martin and Vincent crouched, examining a strange occurrence.

"What is it?" James asked, having assumed a place in the front.

Martin turned as Vincent held up the end of a rope placed upon the ground, matching the exact pattern and manufacture as the other end in Martin's grasp.

They were back at the beginning of their journey.

XXIV

"This is impossible," William muttered.

"We cannot have been walking in a circle," James added.

Martin and Vincent stayed crouched, uncertain of what to make of the situation.

"The pathway is straight, at no time were we walking along a curve," Robert bolstered.

"I feel we are being toyed with," Martin spoke just loud enough for Vincent to hear beside him. He was reassured by a knowing and wordless nod by his captain as he rose. As he stood, Vincent took hold of Martin's end of the rope. It extended exactly to its beginning. This was no coincidence.

"We are being led back to the stone door," Robert expressed.

"It is the only way for us to escape this place," Christopher agreed.

Inwardly, Vincent knew their sentiments to hold validity. He also strained against the merciless advent of fate that had gripped their actions as of late.

"It seems that for now we must adhere to the avenue open to us," the captain stated in resignation. Leaving the rope where it lay, he led the seven back toward the cavern as the Damascus Sword seemed to approve of the decision and began growing in brightness as they approached.

Christopher and Robert were the first to enter and touch the mysterious stone plate. All surrounded the artifact, uncertain of how to best proceed.

"When we experienced the effect, it was a floating sensation, without sound or breath," Vincent attempted to explain to the growing tension he felt about him.

"It is the only way," Robert emphasized, his abstract curiosity and interest certainly clouding his judgment.

"It will be important that we all hold to each other as we attempt to travel to another point," Diana, the most experienced in the group, expounded. "We will see four stars, and must make a decision quickly and move toward one of them."

"It stands to reason that one of the four stars represents this location," Martin provided.

"In that case, we must try again," Vincent answered. "Not only our escape from here, but also the advancement of our goal must be accomplished through this portal."

The unspoken question was aired by James.

"What if we lose contact?"

Vincent looked to Diana.

"We do not know," she admitted. "When I . . . lost my father leaving the prison . . ."

"We simply cannot know the consequences," Vincent completed.

A moment of silence steeled resolve within the seven.

"We stand by you and your judgment," William proclaimed, standing behind Diana and facing the stone door. Each of the others did likewise as Vincent held the shining sword outward.

Reaching out, just as he had done earlier upon discovering the stone's unknown properties, Vincent made contact with the cold surface and felt a pull. He was able to resist the force at first, but it grew in strength. He turned to call out to the others, but his voice failed him. Martin was at his side and Diana directly behind as they were drawn inward. The others, intertwined by arms and elbows, fell forward and in the span of a breath the seven were cast into the oblivion of the airless and soundless expanse.

The repulsing force tore the seven apart the instant they had crossed the plane. What Vincent had understood earlier when he and Diana had held firmly to the blade rang true again. It was difficult in that situation for two individuals to maneuver the expanse before holding firm to the Damascus Sword; seven individuals proved impossible to coordinate in the wordless vacuum.

Martin was first to disappear, pushed distant with a power Vincent could not resist or affect. As the captain spun soundlessly, Damascus Sword in hand, he saw only Diana cleft firmly to his left ankle, the others fragmenting from the group and vanishing with horror written across their countenances.

The four stars were present, undulating in the distance, but Vincent's energy and attention were spent entirely on keeping the only remnant of the group attached to the sword. He felt the force pushing them apart as before, but as he calmed his senses Vincent realized that the sensation was different this time. The Damascus Sword was not pulling them *apart*, but seeking out *Diana*.

Try as he might, Vincent could not maintain his hold on the blade. Diana scaled upward, never losing contact, and reached out to aid him as before. The Damascus Sword flew to her outstretched hand and Vincent was flung clear by its irresistible push. Their eyes locked in wide terror, then all faded away.

Where is he?
Vincent opened his eyes.
He has arrived.
Sound returned to his ears. Breath to his lungs.
He is awake.
Vincent moved his arms and legs. As though waking from a deep sleep, his tendons and sinews strained and stretched.
Do not exert yourself.
He was alone. He knew this without looking about. Ears registered voices.
Two voices.
Two female voices.
There is no return now.
Blue sky greeted his eyes. He was lying on his back. On grass.
Real grass.
He lifted his head. Legs and arms moved slowly, but obediently.
He stood.
Vincent was standing in a graveyard. He knew the place well.

A figure stood before him, facing away. This was the origin of one of the voices, Vincent knew. He also understood that in some unknown way the voice's identity was familiar.

This was not the first time.

"I knew you before you could comprehend," the figure spoke.

A large and ornate gravestone stood between them. He knew it at once. It was the stone of Lord West's late wife, Diana's mother, deceased for some time now.

He was in the Ballecetine graveyard.

Vincent looked about, knowing before that he was alone but needing his senses to confirm the fact.

"You are the source, and the end," the female continued as she turned to face Vincent.

A robe the color of flame adhered to her tall frame. Blackness surrounded her face and eyes deeper than the purest emerald peered through his soul. Vincent took a dangerous step forward to face the impossible. His eyes could not look away from what he knew could not be.

"Welcome home, Vincent, my son," she spoke.

The face of one he had never seen called out from within his memory. The voice he had never heard while he drew breath stirred his heart within. His mouth formed the word both kindred and alien.

"Mother."